CROOKED MAN

"This is a terrific first novel . . . a rich, funny, textured story of life in the New Orleans demimonde . . . a wonderful cast of supporting characters . . . Dunbar has an excellent ear for dialogue, and his story is very well crafted. His stylish take on Big Easy lowlife is reminiscent of the best of Donald Westlake and Elmore Leonard. This book deserves a wide and enthusiastic readership; don't miss it!"
—*Booklist*

"*Crooked Man* is the literary equivalent of a *film noir*—fast, tough, tense, and darkly funny, and with an ending so deeply satisfying in the settling of the story's several scores that a reader might well disturb the midnight silence with laughter."
—*Los Angeles Times Book Review*

"A deliciously witty caper through the idiosyncratic landscape of New Orleans with a conclusion that's as cleverly convoluted and amusing as the rest of this tale."
—*Publishers Weekly*

"The sense of place in *Crooked Man* is so thick you can smell the chicory in the French roast coffee . . . Tubby may have gone into this adventure as 'the sweetest little lawyer in New Orleans,' but he comes out of it with the savvy to play this slippery game like a pro."
—*New York Times Book Review*

"A stellar debut. Tony Dunbar's New Orleans and its vast array of characters are as crisp as fried catfish, as tasty as soft-shelled crab."
—Joe Gores, Egdar Award-winning author of *32 Cadillacs* and *Dead Man*

Berkley Prime Crime Books by Tony Dunbar

CITY OF BEADS
TRICK QUESTION

trick question

tony dunbar

BERKLEY PRIME CRIME, NEW YORK

This book is fiction. All of these characters and settings
are purely imaginary. There is no Tubby Dubonnet and the real
New Orleans is different from his make-believe city.

TRICK QUESTION

A Berkley Prime Crime Book / published by arrangement with
the author

PRINTING HISTORY
G. P. Putnam's Sons hardcover edition / 1996
Berkley Prime Crime mass-market edition / November 1997

The Putnam Berkley World Wide Web site address is
http://www.berkley.com

ISBN: 0-425-16092-0

Berkley Prime Crime Books are published
by The Berkley Publishing Group,
200 Madison Avenue, New York NY 10016
The name BERKLEY PRIME CRIME and the BERKLEY PRIME
CRIME design are trademarks belonging to Berkley Publishing
Corporation

PRINTED IN THE UNITED STATES OF AMERICA

10 9 8 7 6 5 4 3 2 1

My special thanks to Mary Abell, M.D., David Flockhart, M.D., and Laurie A. White, Esq., for their good-natured comments about how greatly incidents in this book differ from the real world of medicine and boxing; to Linda Kravitz, Kristin Lindstrom, and Heather Kennedy for reading early drafts and being generous with their criticism, and to Carrie Lee Pierson for translating this from a long-lost computer language into a modern dialect.

for mary price
i'm a different man

trick question

chapter 1

Traffic was light. It usually was on the old Highway 11 bridge across Lake Pontchartrain from Slidell to New Orleans. Most everyone traveled the interstate nowadays. Its straight concrete spans were visible in the distance, but if you were coming in from the fishing camps on the north-shore, as Wheezy Wascomb was, the old bridge was the shortest way to the city. She was driving to town to pick up her grandchildren and take them back out to the lake for the weekend. They were at the age when going fishing for crabs off a creaking wooden dock was just about the best fun they could imagine. A light breeze carried the smell of salt from the Gulf of Mexico, and the sunshine flashing off her fenders made Wheezy squint.

The bridge was long and narrow, built sometime around World War II when they were just learning to pour lots of concrete and everybody drove slower cars. They must have designed the roadway for midgets, too, because when a pickup truck cruising at a steady seventy zoomed past Wheezy's little Toyota, her car blew about three feet toward the battered gray stone-and-clamshell barrier. Her heart raced almost painfully as she watched the pickup fly away with a throaty roar from its chrome pipes. Truth was, she had been feeling light-headed ever since she got into the car. She had not been well all week. Those Endflu capsules, promising eight hours of relief without drowsiness, had been keeping her upright, but this morning she was feeling positively awful.

Suddenly she found it hard to breathe. A car coming at her out of the bright sunlight had to honk to shove her back into her lane. She fought to control the steering, but the bridge itself seemed to twist in front of her eyes. Sweat poured out of her and a dark red curtain fell down over her field of view. She was too scared to scream. Sparklers began going off in her head.

She hit the concrete rail at forty-five miles per hour, and the determined Toyota tried to climb over it. The metal peeled away and the frame in front collapsed loudly in a rainstorm of sparks, but the old barricade held. The crushed Toyota spun once and rolled over on its side, blocking the highway. One tire rotated furiously, and fluids, purple and orange, poured dangerously onto the pavement. Wheezy Wascomb was dumped on the floor—her heart had burst.

chapter 2

Moskowitz Memorial Laboratory is the last stop for lots of mice and hamsters, and now and then a monkey. It is one of the planet's foremost facilities for isolating the things that make people swell up and die, and for wiping them out. It is a source of pride and not insignificant profit for its mother ship, the highly regarded New Orleans State University Medical School.

Most of the time the place is hopping with an irreverent crew of doctors and their research assistants, wearing white coats over their faded blue jeans and sneakers. But on Sunday night it is fairly quiet, except for the shuffling of white, furry rodents in their hutches, making little sounds in antiseptic cages.

They became still for a moment when the door to the animal care laboratory slid open, sucking a puff of cool air out into the hallway before the seal was restored. Cletus Busters, the custodian, trudged in, tugging behind him his cart full of brooms and mops and the bags of trash he had collected as he made his way from room to room. He parked the cart by the door and, with an air of innocence, wandered around the lab without any apparent objective in mind.

"Hello, little rat," he whispered, brushing the front of

one of the metal cages with his fingers. The occupant twisted its nose at him and flicked a long whisker.

Cletus surreptitiously opened a drawer in one of the stainless steel counters that ran the length of the room and poked around inside. He checked the labels on several of the bottles he found there and then put them back as they were. He looked around the room and pretended to whistle a tune.

A white-enameled, closet-sized door attracted his attention. It was kind of like the narrow cover of a ship's hatch. There was a big red-lettered sign taped to it which he did not have much trouble reading. His lips moved as he worked it out: SAMPLES/CAREFUL. Below that someone had written in pencil, maybe as a joke, "Dressing Room—No Peeking." Above the sign there was a small round glass gauge that registered interior temperature in degrees centigrade. It was fixed at minus 180.

Cletus sneaked a backwards glance toward the sliding door where he had left his cart, and then he grabbed the cold chrome handle of the closet with both hands and gave it a good pull.

Harsh cold air blew around him, and the dead man inside came out.

The body teetered, hard and solid as a statue, and fell directly at Cletus. He jumped back in terror, gasping, and the head missed striking him by an inch. The corpse's frost-bitten eyes grabbed at Cletus's in passing, glinting with recognition and accusation it seemed to him, but then sailed past, and it didn't matter. The body smacked against the white-tiled floor with the sound a 175-pound ice cube might make.

On impact it did an atrocious thing. The head snapped off and flipped into the air, making another pass at Cletus. He dodged, choking a scream, and it bounced a few feet away, coming to rest at the base of a steel hotel full of hamsters. The dead eyes, oblivious to the squeals and panic they had caused, stared blankly at the ceiling. A mustache on the face, like a graffiti smudge on a marble sculpture, was fuzzy with ice crystals.

Cletus smashed spread-eagled in fright against a rack of rat cages, his fingers grasping the wire mesh for support. The animals inside cowered. He recovered slightly and crouched down to inspect the object at his feet.

"Dr. Valentine!" he exclaimed.

He grabbed the head and crawled over the tiled floor to try to stick it back on the shoulders where it belonged, right where a frozen nub of bone protruded from the stiff white lab coat.

The piece wouldn't fit the puzzle. His hands shaking, Cletus lifted the frosty head to stare again into those glacial eyes. Then, cradling it like a football, he rushed back to his cart to find some cleaning rags to wrap it in. He hit the silver plate to make the door slide open.

"Anything wrong here?" asked the security guard. "I thought I heard some noise."

Cletus just looked at him, breathing hard and licking his lips.

The guard took a step forward. He peered past Cletus. His eyes roamed the lab. Then they moved downward to see what Cletus had in his arms, and grew wide with interest.

chapter 3

Victory is the reward for perseverance, that was Jason Boaz's theme. Three races into the afternoon and he was finally waving a winning ticket into the air.

"Blue Femme! What a doll!" he shouted into Tubby's ear. He waved his arms exuberantly, forcing people out of his path.

"I'm happy for you," Tubby grumbled. He tore up his ticket to place on Nutria Challenger, the horse that had come in fourth, and scattered the pieces on the grandstand steps.

It was a sunny winter afternoon, fading toward evening. The crowd milled about while the horses were led away and trainers ran around preparing for the next race. Both Jason and Tubby had dates, so to speak, but the ladies had retired to the clubhouse half an hour earlier after the initial thrill of the Fairgrounds had worn off.

"Let's go collect my dough and find the babes," Jason said happily, and Tubby followed him up the steps. He left Jason in the line to cash in and headed off toward the bar. He fancied that he cut a nice figure. Healthy enough, tanned, with blond hair cut maybe a little bit too long for a lawyer, he felt good about the way he was holding up—even forty-something years into the game. Maybe there were a few extra ounces padding his broad frame, but he could still suit up for tennis. He still looked at home behind the wheel of his sports car.

His companion for the day was Jynx Margolis, lately divorced, and flush with the bucks of her former husband, the gynecologist. And his friend, the local inventor Jason Boaz, had brought Norella Peruna, recently of Honduras, who had fudge-colored skin, gleaming white teeth, and a pink hibiscus in her raven hair. The women were head to head over margaritas, framed by the window with the blue sky and the snapping pennants of the racetrack as their backdrop. Lovely, lovely, Tubby thought.

"You two make a very pretty picture," he said admiringly.

"Why thank you, Mr. Dubonnet," Jynx said, her smile sparkling, patting the chair beside her. Tubby sat down gratefully and waved at the waitress.

"Did you win lots of of money?" Norella asked.

"Jason did," Tubby said. "I'm not the lucky one today."

"You've had me for the afternoon," Jynx pointed out.

"That I have," Tubby acknowledged. "What would you ladies like to drink?"

Jynx said she could stand another margarita, Norella said she couldn't, and Tubby ordered a gin and tonic for himself.

"Are you having fun ignoring the races?" he asked.

"Oh, yes." Norella beamed.

"I had no idea watching horses could be so much fun," Jynx said.

Tubby was going to say something sarcastic, but Jason came upon them, making loud noises about winning money, the science of equestrian spirit, and the hunch he had about any horse with a French name.

They toasted his success, and Tubby was about to suggest wagering on the next race when Jason announced that they should all leave and go to the Belle o' the Ball Casino out by the lake to play blackjack with his money.

"My treat," he exclaimed. "Everybody gets a stake. After you run through that, you'll have to just sit and drink.''

"We can keep our winnings?" Norella asked.

"Half is mine," Jason said. "That's the deal."

"That would be fun," his Latin beauty said gaily.

"Oh, I don't think so," Jynx said. "I have to be home by six o'clock. I have a club meeting at my house tomorrow and I need to straighten the place up and plan the menu."

Tubby said he was following Jynx, because he was a gentleman, and because he had never liked to go into crowded rooms to place a bet.

Norella and Jynx went to the powder room to talk it over.

"You're involved with the Casino Mall Grandé in some way, aren't you?" Jason asked.

"How do you mean, involved?"

"I thought you did some of their legal work."

"That never really developed," Tubby said evasively. "I thought I was going to get some business, but it didn't come through. To tell you the truth, I'm not sad about it. I love to gamble, you know that, but something about the whole casino atmosphere just isn't me, I guess."

"I didn't know you turned clients away, Tubby."

"Well, actually, I didn't turn them away," Tubby admitted. "My contact there, Jake LaBreau, left and . . ." He shrugged. His other contact, Nicole Normande, had been transferred to Arizona, and her brother, Leo Caspar . . . well, Leo had been whacked into little bits and fed to the fish. Tubby grimaced.

"What's LaBreau doing now?" Jason asked.

"Promoting the idea of a theme park out in Chalmette."

"Mosquito-World? Crawfish-World?" Jason suggested, referring to the most plentiful inhabitants of "the parish."

"You're such a snob. No, jazz, I think. Whatever the politicians think sounds good."

"What the hell, let's go play a few hands anyway. And I ain't a snob. I married a Chalmatian once."

"And she had the good sense to run home to mama, but if Jynx wants to go, it's okay with me."

"She's got the hots for you." Jason leered and socked Tubby's shoulder.

"You think so?" Tubby was hopeful.

"Absolutely. All that stuff about going home early. She's got something special planned for you."

"Hey, maybe so."

The women returned, and the party got moving.

Out in the parking lot Jason helped Norella into his Lexus, but Jynx remained firm about going home. Jason gave Tubby a wink and sped away.

Tubby and Jynx got into his restored Lincoln with the fake convertible top, which he had bought to give his Corvair Spyder a big brother in the driveway, and set out toward uptown. It was a nice evening, and Jynx chattered away all the way down Broad Street about how colorful the Fairgrounds Racetrack was and how she couldn't believe she had lived her whole life in New Orleans and never once seen the horses run before.

He turned into her driveway, and she gave him another big smile.

"Thank you for a lovely time," she said as he pushed the shifter into park. "I would invite you in for a drink, but the place is such a mess. Dorene has been sick, and it looks like little ol' me is going to have to clean it up all by myself."

"You need some help?" Tubby offered, trying to be nonchalant.

"You're such a dear, but I certainly can't ask you to vacuum my house. I'll let you help me some other time with something you can do."

"Like, uh, what?" Tubby was asking, but Jynx was out of the car and waving goodbye from her doorstep.

Friday night, and he was on his own again.

chapter 4

Tubby Dubonnet had been the proud proprietor of Mike's Bar for about three months, but he hadn't changed it much. From the outside it was still the same nondescript place, advertised only by a faded Falstaff beer sign hanging from a rusty iron rod above the door. Weeds still grew on the curbs, and trash can lids still blew down Annunciation Street in the Irish Channel. Kids played in the sunshine on the sidewalks outside. At night the people kept their doors open and watched TV. The bar had no windows, just a one-way glass in the front door so the bartender could see who wanted to come in before he pushed the buzzer that worked the lock.

"Two down, one up," the dealer at the table in the back announced. "King bets," she said.

"Thirty cents," said Judge Duzet.

"And fifty," said Mrs. Pearl.

"Feeling good," the dealer said. "How about you?"

"I'm in." Rodney sighed.

Coins clinked against each other on the table.

Tubby, sitting at the bar, put Jynx Margolis out of his mind as he listened to the betting and smiled. Raisin Partlow, his buddy, held down the stool next to his. Raisin had a pretty good head of curly black hair and what you would call a mature, rugged look. Women liked him—and he hardly ever worked, which made him an easy guy to pal around with. He followed Tubby's gaze across the room.

"What are you grinning about?" he asked.

" 'Cause the same crowd is still coming to the ol' bar even though Mr. Mike isn't around anymore," Tubby said. "I'm pretty happy about that."

"I wouldn't exactly call it a crowd, Tubby, and they don't seem to be drinking all that much either."

"This isn't about money, Raisin. This is about tradition and continuity. Look around you." The sweep of Tubby's arm took in the trophies above the bar, earned by softball teams of years past; the team photographs on the wall signed by old baseball players; the jukebox, now playing Louis Prima; and Larry, the ghostly bartender hidden in the shadows beside the cashbox.

"It's a monument, all right," Raisin agreed. "How come you don't ever sit in the nice chair?"

He meant the worn leather armchair at the card table, where Mike, the previous owner, had held court.

"Maybe when I retire," Tubby said. "For now it's reserved for Mr. Mike, whenever he drags in. In fact, I'm thinking of having a little plaque made up and hanging it there."

"Like the Half Moon Bar used to have? 'This table reserved for Victor Bussie, AFL-CIO'?"

"Yeah. It could say: 'Reserved for Mr. Mike when he isn't fishing.' "

The door buzzer sounded, and Larry's arm emerged from the darkness to press a button.

Tubby and Raisin both turned around and watched a tall thin man in a rumpled suit, silhouetted by the lights of a passing car, enter unsteadily. He paused to let his eyes adjust to the perpetual dimness of Mike's, and then he made his uncertain way to a stool at the far end of the bar.

"Don't I know him?" Raisin asked Tubby.

"Yeah. That's Mickey O'Rourke. He was in law school about ten years before I was. I know you've noticed him around. But Christ, he's seen better days."

"He don't look like he's doing too good," Raisin agreed.

"He had a couple of big cases a long time ago, like real big. He won one of the first seven-figure judgments we had around here. I haven't heard much about him lately though."

"Tubby Dubonnet," O'Rourke exclaimed. He got off his stool and, gripping the large glass of Scotch and something Larry had just served him, weaved down the bar to say hello.

His tie was loose and he smelled of whiskey and cigarette smoke, as if he had been taking his meals in a tavern. The lines on his face turned to deep creases when he grinned at Tubby and grasped his hand.

"Howya doin', Mickey? You know my friend, Raisin Partlow?"

"Raisin? Good to meet you. Tubby's friends are all good people." He pumped Raisin's hand. "What y'all drinking? I'm buying."

"Wild Turkey on the rocks," Raisin said.

Tubby waved, and Larry floated over to take their orders. He checked Tubby, who nodded to indicate he wanted his usual for this week, a Barq's root beer and lime. He was experimenting with various nonalcoholic combinations in an effort to cut his toxicity level a little.

"It's been a while," Tubby said. "What's been happening to you?"

"Things have not been too good. My wife left me. My kids won't return my calls. I've been drinking all the time. I lost my house, and my law practice has just about dried up." Mickey knocked back whatever he had in his glass and signaled the barkeep for another. "I think that sums it up."

"Gee, that's too bad," Tubby said.

"How's your dog?" Raisin asked.

Mickey studied Raisin. "I like your friend," he said, putting his arm around Raisin's shoulder and giving it a hug.

"Lemme tell you a joke," O'Rourke said. "See, this Jewish guy goes into the church, right? He goes into the confessional. 'Padre,' he says, 'I went out last night with this beautiful twenty-two-year-old girl. She's gorgeous. Looks like Jodie Foster, whatever. And I got laid, Father. It was great.'

" 'Mr. Katz, why are you telling me this?' the priest says. 'You're Jewish.'

" 'You don't understand, Father. I'm telling everybody!' "

They all laughed.

"But seriously," Mickey said, "my life is hell."

"You think it might have something to do with the booze?" Tubby asked casually.

O'Rourke nodded—no argument there.

"You should maybe try giving it a rest," Tubby suggested. "There are lots of programs."

"I'm a lush, Tubby." Mickey was sad. "It's got ahold of me deep down. There's no use me trying to quit."

"That's bullshit, of course," Tubby said. "I've seen you in the courtroom. I know you can control yourself."

There was a sudden spurt of laughter and groaning from the table in the corner. Mrs. Randazzo in her black wig slapped her cards down and cackled.

"I just got where I don't want to do it anymore." Mickey sat down on the stool. His shoulders slumped. He turned away from them and rubbed his eyes. Tubby and Raisin exchanged glances.

"Take it easy, man," Tubby said. He patted O'Rourke lightly on the back.

Mickey swiveled around.

"I need your help, Tubby," he said, almost sobbing.

"Sure, Mickey. What can I do?"

Raisin rolled his eyes.

"I'm in a situation. I got a trial in a week. It's a murder trial. And I don't have the faintest idea what my defense is. You understand me?"

"No," Tubby said.

"I'm telling you I'm defending a man for murder, and I haven't done a fucking thing." Mickey's eyes were wide open. He was frightened.

Tubby was shocked. "You ought to withdraw or something, Mickey. You might do some serious damage to your client. You could get disbarred for that."

Mickey nodded his head. He knew.

"Have you talked to the judge about this?"

"Yes, and the son of a bitch won't let me out. Tubby, I need help. You're a good trial lawyer. Be a pal, will you?"

"No way," Tubby said.

"Bravo!" Raisin roared.

Mickey gripped Tubby's arm. "It's like a gift from God running into you, Tubby. Everybody I know avoids me. You're a good lawyer, a great lawyer. I can't do this alone. I'm a fucking drunk, for Christ's sake."

"Mickey, there's no way for me to drop everything and jump into some murder trial at the last minute. It would be malpractice."

"Look, Tubby, I could pay you."

"Really?" Tubby was doubtful. "How much?"

"A whole lot. Whatever you say. My Aunt Anne, bless her heart, is gonna kick the bucket any day now. She's gonna leave me a bundle. I'll be able to take care of you then."

Tubby was insulted. "That's ridiculous, Mickey. That's the kind of thing some poor guy in Central Lockup would try to put over on me."

Mickey shrugged his sad shoulders and studied the last of his ice cubes. "Yeah, you're right." He squinted and turned to face Tubby. "But you owe me." His voice was raspy.

"Owe you! For what?" Tubby exclaimed.

"It was me"—O'Rourke pointed at his sunken chest—"who introduced you to Mattie."

"Jesus," Tubby barked. "Mattie left me, in case you didn't know. I should show you all the bills I got for marriage counseling. Maybe you want to pay those."

O'Rourke shook his head. He took his glass and drained it. Then he stood up and brushed imaginary crumbs off his chest.

"I understand, Tubby. See you around."

With dignity, he took a wobbly path toward the front door.

Tubby watched him go.

"Shit," he muttered. "Hey, Mickey," he called.

Mickey halted and rotated.

"Sleep it off. Call me in the morning. If you remember to do that, I'll have lunch with you and we can talk about your problem."

Mickey saluted and banged out the door.

"Can you believe this guy?" Raisin asked the bar. "Tubby, you should have been a priest."

"I'm a Protestant," Tubby said, and sipped his root beer and lime.

"So you think you owe this guy something?"

"Hell no," Tubby said. He thought about what the last year with his ex-wife had been like—the life of the walking dead. Then he remembered his first encounter with her on Mickey's yacht, back when Mickey was flush. Mattie, buxom and redheaded, full of herself in a white cotton dress blowing in the wind, had given him her special smile from across the deck, and his life had changed. Together they had brought three children into the world. The way he cared for them was a secret thing. Maybe he did owe Mickey.

"I'll just talk to him tomorrow and figure something out. We'll get the trial postponed."

"What do you think of that story about his rich Aunt Anne?" Raisin asked.

"It's gonna snow Big Shot soda on St. Charles Avenue in August," Tubby replied.

chapter 5

"How was your weekend?" the lawyer behind Tubby in the elevator asked the person next to him.

"Nice," a woman replied. "We spent Saturday in Pass Christian. But the traffic. It's all the casinos. Lord, what a mess."

"It's really too bad," the man agreed. "Gambling has just about destroyed the Gulf Coast."

What is he talking about? Tubby wondered. The world's funkiest, most hurricane-blasted, totally man-made beach could not be much damaged by the bright lights of dockside gambling. His recent experiences representing a mob-infested and now defunct New Orleans casino might have soured him on the industry, but jeez, gimme a break. Ruin the Mississippi Gulf Coast?

The elevator door opened and he stood aside to let the couple pass. Both of them were well scrubbed and attractive, both carrying bulky briefcases, full of weighty legal matters.

The doors slid shut, and Tubby ascended to the forty-third floor. Out the doors, two right turns, and he reached the offices of Dubonnet & Associates, designated in large gold letters on a pair of solid maple doors.

Inside, Cherrylynn looked up from her desk.

"Morning, boss," she called cheerfully. "Good to see you."

Was she being sarcastic? She made a little fun of the hours he'd been keeping lately, and he was getting sensitive. It seemed to have placed some kind of a strain on his secretary that he was not working overtime every day.

"Lots of messages for you. I put them on your desk. How's the bar business?"

Now he knew she was being sarcastic.

"Just fine," Tubby said stiffly, and went into his office. Cherrylynn was a mite wild herself, at age twenty-six, but over the past three years working for Tubby she had decided that one of her functions was assuring that he stayed on a straight and narrow course. She could be a pain, but he realized that he probably needed a pain like her around sometimes.

He liked his office. Its best features were the simple wooden desk and the window through which he could see most of the universe he cared about—the cracked tile roofs of the historic buildings in the French Quarter, the steady bustle of Canal Street, ships navigating the hairpin bend of the Mississippi River, and a thousand blocks of old neighborhoods stretching away to the seawall around Lake Pontchartrain. He could make out the sails of a few pleasure boats and started imagining what a day of fishing for his supper would feel like. Right now a morning rainstorm was breaking up over the Industrial Canal, dark clouds thinning out to blue, while downtown the sun shone on office workers shuffling miserably along the sidewalks.

"Knock, knock," Cherrylynn said from the doorway. Tubby reluctantly stepped back from the window.

"Can I ask you a question, boss?"

"Sure," he said, taking off his coat and dropping it on one of the two armchairs facing his desk. "You want to sit down?"

She lowered herself gently onto the other chair, smoothing out her dress underneath.

"This feels like I'm a client," she giggled. She had freckles, and they blended together when she did that.

Tubby had described his secretary as "pert," a quality she had brought with her from Puget Sound. She had a well-scrubbed north woods glow that set her apart from many a well-powdered New Orleans lady, but she liked to smile, which looked right at home in the city that care forgot. She complained that she had a drawerful of sweaters and nowhere to wear them. There had once been an oilfield roustabout in her life, a boyfriend or maybe even a boy-husband. Cherrylynn didn't talk about him, but she maintained an unlisted phone number.

Tubby took his familiar place behind the desk and folded his hands on its well-worn top of ruddy cypress. He looked at her benignly.

"What's up?"

"Okay," she began seriously. "I didn't say anything when you bought the bar." That wasn't true. "But now you've had it a couple of months, and it seems to me you're spending more and more time over there, like every afternoon."

"Are you worrying about me drinking too much?"

"I always worry about that, but that's really your business, boss. I just want to know how I fit in and what the future holds."

"What do you mean?"

"Like, are you thinking about closing down your law practice, or anything like that? Should I be looking around for a new job?"

Tubby thought a moment before he answered. Had things really gotten so bad?

"No," he said finally. "I think I'm stuck with being a lawyer. I'll be honest with you. I get tired of all the conflict sometimes and like to dream about just lying out on a beach chair, sipping exotic fluids and watching the waves roll in. But I think I'm not ready to retire yet. I like being involved in people's lives too much."

"Yeah, I know you're that way," Cherrylynn agreed. "You're good at talking to people. I just wondered if maybe you weren't getting all the conversation you needed at Mike's Bar."

Tubby smiled. "I get plenty there, all right. But the relationship I have with people as a lawyer is a lot different than a bartender has. Being a lawyer is like a holy trust, Cherrylynn. That sounds like bull, I know, but when a client tells me something it's private, and no judge can make me divulge my clients' secrets. Let's just say I don't always like what I do, but I still love the profession. I'm not about to close up shop as long as I can pay the rent."

"Okay," Cherrylynn said.

"And one reason I can leave early in the afternoon is because I have you to rely on, so I hope you stick around."

"I don't have any plans to leave, Mr. D." Cherrylynn was glowing. She popped up. "That's all I wanted to know," she said, dancing out.

Tubby waved goodbye to her. How much of that was true? he asked himself. Did he really think it was a holy trust? He had forgotten most of the zillion ethical rules he had once sworn to uphold, but he did believe you should never screw a client. And never lie to the judge. And always try to get paid. That was holy enough for him.

Tubby forced himself to look at the pile of mail Cherrylynn had stacked neatly by the telephone.

He found a couple of bills, which he glared at and tossed back into her box to take care of later. And an interesting square pink envelope with his address neatly written in a childlike hand.

He tore it open and found:

                                              Sunday
Dear Mr. Dubonnet,

How are you? I am writing because a friend of mine has a problem. Her name is Denise DiMaggio. And it involves her father's business. She will tell you about it. She has lots of problems.

I told her she could call you. I hope you don't mind. She doesn't have a lot of money, but I might be able to help pay your fee.

Everything is going fine with me. Lisa is in school

in Lakecrest Elementary and likes New Orleans. She is making friends and is happy to be with me. I will always be grateful to you for getting her back for me. If I ever have another child, I will name him Tubby if it is a boy. I don't know what if it's a girl.

I would like for you to come out and see us sometimes.

Love Always,
Monique Alvarez

Tubby read the letter again and got a bit misty-eyed. Such a nice girl, Monique. A sweetheart. She ran a bar called Champs. Her boyfriend, Darryl Alvarez, had been shot to death right by the cash register. Monique had seen the whole thing. Then she took over the bar, and apparently Darryl's last name as well, which was news to Tubby. He kept meaning to drop in and see how she was doing. He liked Monique because she had grit.

He buckled down to work, running through his mail, marking his upcoming court appearances on his calendar, and reading with mounting irritation a bogus set of eight exceptions an opposing counsel had filed to delay and obstruct a perfectly legitimate lawsuit Tubby had filed to assert his client's right to a family fortune.

"I'm having lunch today with Mickey O'Rourke," Tubby told Cherrylynn on the way out the door. "Can I bring you anything from Ditcharo's?"

"Nope, I brought my nuke food," Cherrylynn called, referring to her Weight Watchers microwave casserole of low-cal glop.

"Ugh," he muttered, and walked to the elevator thinking about fried oysters. The Ricca family did a great job with any kind of seafood, stewed chicken, stuffed peppers, any kind of regular food you could name. Just what Mickey needed to soak up all that booze. They kept the place simple. No fancy art on the walls, just a few letters from the fans. The menu hanging over the counter hardly ever changed, and instead of decor, the restaurant offered the kind of aroma that made you want to push the guy ahead of you out of line.

But Mickey was late. Tubby was starting on the second half of his muffaletta, immensely enjoying the spicy olive salad, ham, and salami in the crusty Italian roll, and reading about Tulane basketball in the *Times-Picayune* sports section, when O'Rourke, looking winded, finally made an appearance.

"Sorry to be late," he said. "My car battery died."

"No problem, Mickey. Go get some lunch. I'll wait."

"Maybe a little something. My stomach has been acting up." He went to the counter and came back with a mug of coffee.

"You should eat," Tubby said, concerned.

"Yeah, I know, but I don't have much of an appetite. I think it's all the pressure I've been under. I can't remember it ever being like this before."

"You probably never hit the bottle so hard before."

"There's been a few other times . . ." Mickey's voice trailed off.

A guy with a tray full of sandwiches and gumbo backed into their table and apologized for spilling O'Rourke's coffee, but Mickey didn't seem to notice.

"About your murder trial, Mickey. You told Judge Stifflemire your problem, and he still wouldn't let you withdraw from the case?"

"He wasn't nasty about it." Mickey found a cigarette in his pocket and began tapping it on the table. "They let you smoke in here?" Tubby shrugged. Mickey lit up. "He gave me several reasons. He said whenever he appoints someone in a criminal case, they always try to get out of it, and his policy is to just refuse them all. Then he tells me about the Speedy Trial Act, and how the DA has to get this guy to trial soon or let him go. Then he says to me that as long as a lawyer can breathe and stay awake at least half the time, he thinks the law and the jurisprudence hold him competent to appear in court."

"I think he's right about that." Tubby scooped up a little olive salad that was trying to get away.

"Yeah? Well, then he says, 'Good luck, Mr. O'Rourke. I'm counting on you.' "

"Geez, was he just being an asshole? He didn't give you much relief, did he? When was this?"

"Just last week. And since then it's like I can't concentrate. I know I got a real problem. I'm drinking all the time. Coming here to meet you is like being on a vacation, but I'm going to start drinking as soon as I leave here. I need to be in a hospital somewhere."

"Maybe that's your solution. I don't think you can expect another lawyer to step in this late in the game."

"I know it would be hard. But it's such a weird case."

"What do you mean?"

"Get this. The deceased is frozen—I mean solid—in a damn specimen case at the university hospital. My man opens the door. The corpse comes out, like 'Timber,' and his damn head snaps off and goes rolling around the room like a bowling ball."

"You're kidding me! The head comes off?" There could be some publicity value in this case.

"Is this wild? This is one guy they aren't going to thaw out in a hundred years and bring back to life. He was a rising-star doctor, too. An Irish guy," Mickey added.

"The, uh, stiff?"

"Yeah. Good joke, huh?"

Tubby was thinking that the news media, properly primed, would likely follow this trial very closely.

"Tell me," he asked, "was there anything to your story about inheriting lots of money?"

"Yes and no," Mickey admitted. "Aunt Anne's rich as God, but she ain't sick. She's gonna outlive us both."

Tubby considered that. Of course, showbiz law had its own rewards.

"What did your man do when the head popped off?" he asked.

"He tells me he tried to put the damn thing back on. Picture that. Pick up a frozen head and try to put Humpty

Dumpty together again. I think he ought to get some kind of reward for his heroism.'' Mickey coughed from his cigarette. His face was white with lots of red spots. ''Instead they charge him with murder.''

''Because of . . . why?''

''They say he was pilfering drugs from the hospital. They found some in his house.''

''But why did he kill the doctor?''

''That's where it breaks down into pure speculation. The DA's theory is, the doctor caught him stealing dope and therefore my guy killed him.''

''Then why does he go back later and open the door?''

''Really! There are some holes in their scenario.''

''I can't understand why I never read about this case.''

''It was in the papers and on the news, Tubby. Have you been out of the country?''

''This was in September? It must have been when me and Raisin drove over to Florida. We were gone about a month.''

''That's what *I* need. A long vacation.''

''It helps. Have you done any discovery—looked at the district attorney's evidence and all that?''

Mickey was shaking visibly now. First his shoulders, then his face.

''I haven't done shit. I can't handle this right now. That's why I'm asking you for help.''

Tubby watched the ladies behind the counter dishing out platters of trout and shrimp. He rubbed his chin.

''How far did the head actually roll?'' he asked.

''About eight feet.'' O'Rourke lit up another smoke and squinted at the match.

''Wow!'' Tubby said to no one in particular. This could be a headliner. ''Okay. Get me the file.''

chapter **6**

Tubby got to Compagno's, New Orleans's smallest Italian restaurant, a little later than he had promised. His eldest, Debbie, was already seated at a table in the back, underneath the Loyola and LSU pennants, the oil painting of Al Hirt at the old Sugar Bowl, and the faded black-and-white photographs of Boy Scouts of generations past. Tubby waved at Sal, the owner, who also tended bar, and spread his hands in apology to his daughter.

"I'm sorry, I got held by traffic."

"Hi, Daddy," she said cheerfully. "Don't worry, I've been having a good time." A stuffed artichoke, full of seasoned bread crumbs and tiny shrimp, sat half demolished on the table in front of her. Debbie had always had a good appetite. Tubby had been watching her put away astounding platters of food for twenty years. She had gotten her big shoulders from him, but she managed to stay slim, like her mother.

Tubby sat down and ordered a beer. He liked the ceiling fans, the bull horns over the bar, the Charles Bronson movie playing on the television, the bottles of Crystal hot sauce on the tables—just about everything in this place.

"It never changes," he said happily.

"Remember when we used to all come here on Saturday

nights?'' Debbie recalled, bringing up a good memory of when the family had all been together—before he and Mattie split up.

"Yeah. You never would order anything but lasagna. We could never get you to even try anything else."

"I'm going to have it tonight, too." She laughed. She still wore her brown hair long, and it bounced around when she talked. Tubby's heart filled up.

He grinned.

"What are you looking at?'' she asked.

"Nothing," he said. "So tell me some current events. Did you ever find your mother?"

A few weeks ago Debbie had invited him, her sisters, and Mattie to a "family" dinner to christen Debbie's new apartment. She had hinted that Mattie had some big news to relate, and Tubby had dutifully attended. Mattie, however, had stood them up. They finally decided to eat anyway, but they were worried until she called in about dessert time. Her excuse had been a bad headache. Everybody shrugged—that's Mom. Tubby had been relieved, because he didn't socialize much with Mattie, but he was also oddly disappointed. He had wanted to know what her news was.

Debbie didn't answer because the waiter came.

"Stuffed merlitons," Tubby said. "You know they grow these on the roof over their carport?" He always tried to sample the city's backyard squash when it was in season.

Debbie ordered lasagna.

They went back to work on the artichoke.—

"She's not lost. You ought to talk to her," she said, poking a stray crumb into her mouth with a sensibly manicured nail.

"What for?'' Tubby asked.

"Just to stay in touch," Debbie said enigmatically.

"Sweet pea,'' Tubby explained, "your mother and I stay in touch just as much as we want to. She's doing okay with her life, and I'm doing the best I can with mine. You can't expect more than that."

"Okay. Just a suggestion," Debbie said, and went back to eating.

"I am curious, of course," Tubby said matter-of-factly, "about the latest gossip. Is she dating someone?"

"I thought you didn't want to stay in touch with her."

"I'd just rather do it through you," he said.

"Hah!"

"So tell me," he said.

"Okay. It's no big secret since they're starting to go out in public. She *has* been dating. I thought you would have heard about it by now anyway."

No. Mattie's comings and goings were not exactly headline material.

"Who's the lucky guy?" he asked.

"You know him."

Uh-oh.

"Who is it?" He braced himself.

"Dr. Margolis."

"Byron Margolis? Jynx Margolis's ex-husband?" Tubby yelled. He was temporarily in shock. "That man's a complete turkey."

"Oh, Daddy." Debbie dismissed him.

"No, really. He treated Jynx like dirt, and he hates me like poison."

"That's because you were his wife's divorce lawyer."

"Right, and I had to chase him all over creation to get him to reveal his income and pay up."

"Well, maybe that's why you have a bad opinion of him. He's been very polite to me."

"You've seen him?" Tubby demanded. Was his own daughter a traitor?

"Why yes," she said, surprised. "I didn't think you would mind."

"But . . ." Tubby sputtered. And why should he mind?

"You don't want her to date?" Debbie asked.

"Of course I do," Tubby declared, but he didn't. This would all require more time to digest.

"So? What?" Debbie asked.

"Nothing, I guess," Tubby said more calmly. "I just wonder if he's trying to use your mother to get back at me."

"Because you helped his wife get a divorce? Daddy, maybe you're not quite that important."

Could it be?

"Yeah, you're right," he said. "Look, let's eat."

His merlitons had arrived, pale green receptacles for crabmeat and boiled shrimp. "I could give up red meat," he commented to no one in particular.

"So, to change the subject, how are you?" he asked, savoring a first mouthful.

"So, since you asked, maybe not so good." She picked at her lasagna.

"What's the matter?"

"I'm possibly pregnant."

His fork clattered off the plate and hit the floor.

She was watching him, the humor gone from her eyes.

"Are you going to tell me more?" he asked finally.

"Yes. I'm probably two months pregnant. The father is probably Marcos."

"Probably?" His voice was rising.

"I didn't mean it that way." She blushed. "Marcos is the father. I just don't know if I'm going to have the baby."

"What does Marcos have to say?" Tubby asked, trying to sound calm.

"He says he wants to get married."

"And you?"

"I told him I'd think about it. I'm not sure I know him well enough yet."

"Good God," Tubby said. "You must know him pretty well."

Debbie laughed a little.

Tubby thought about what a young girl she was and what an old man he was, and shook his head.

"I'm not sure he's mature enough to get married," Debbie added.

"You've got some tough decisions to make," was all he could manage to say.

"You used to tell me that's what life's all about," she replied sagely.

His eyes fogged up.

"Is everything all right?" Sal inquired heartily, leaning over the table, his arms and tomato-stained apron like a tent around them, and a big friendly smile on his round face.

As he walked back across the park, all Tubby could think about was children having babies. Was it realistic to think that Debbie could care for a child? She had a good head, some of the time, and a good heart, but where was the money going to come from? Watching all the ladies pushing their colorful strollers around the lagoon, the dads showing their little boys how to toss bread at the ducks, reminded him of all the work involved in raising a baby. He bet he'd end up having to take care of that kid himself.

chapter 7

Flowers looked sleepy.

"I got here as fast as I could," he said. "The message from Cherrylynn was that this was an emergency."

It was after hours, and Tubby was standing over his desk with his sleeves rolled up and his shirt collar open. He had the pieces of the Cletus Busters file spread out, hoping to conjure up some brilliant idea from the scattered notes O'Rourke had managed to collect. When Flowers walked in he was trying to make sense of what Mickey had jotted down about Cletus finding the body.

He shook Flowers's oversized hand. People thought of Tubby as big, but Flowers was bigger. And younger, taller, darker, handsomer, and in better shape. Flowers, whose real name was Sanré Fueres, worked out regularly, as befitted his image as a macho, ex-FBI, big-city private investigator. Why is a barely-thirty-year-old man "ex-FBI"? Tubby had never asked.

"Thanks for coming."

"You call, I'm here. Have you got a new case for me?"

"Yes, and a very interesting one."

"I'm glad to hear it. I've been staking out a young woman's apartment in Slidell for two days trying to get photographs of her boyfriend. I think he's in there, but he's not coming up for air. You think they're having a party?''

"He probably came out as soon as you left.''

"I hope so, 'cause my man Charlie is waiting down the street with the big Nikon three-hundred-millimeter lens.''

"You lead an exciting life, Flowers.''

"Too exciting. Last week I was watching this house trailer on Chef Menteur Highway, and this guy came flying out with a damn shotgun. I got careless and he spotted me. He comes charging across the lawn in his underwear like he's hitting the beach on D-Day.''

"What did you do?''

"I peeled rubber. Hit the road, Jack. Gone pecan. I had my old Cherokee around the corner and out of sight in about one and a half seconds, and I haven't been back. I got a good picture of him though, crashing out the door and pumping shells in his gun.''

"The neighbors must have gotten quite an eyeful.''

"They were running for cover, sure enough.'' Flowers laughed.

"Well, now I need you for some real investigative work. I've got a murder trial coming up in a week, unless I can get it postponed, and I've got to prepare my case virtually from scratch.''

"What do you want me to do?''

"Pull up a chair and start taking notes.''

Flowers took a leather-covered notebook from the pocket of his Saints windbreaker and sat. The old chair creaked.

Tubby stood looking out the window at the ring of city lights that marked the shoreline of Lake Pontchartrain at night, and he started talking.

"The victim is a doctor at New Orleans Medical Center. His name is Whitney Valentine. He's what they call a research pathologist. He finds special diseases nobody ever heard of and figures out what makes them kill people, that sort of thing. He lived here in New Orleans for five years, and he graduated from Tulane. Originally he's from Seattle. He's got a wife in the suburbs.

"My client is a nobody—a janitor at the medical center. He's been there three years. Evidently he has a prior from selling crack or something. They didn't know about that when he was hired. Every night he cleans up the labs, including the one where Dr. Valentine worked. Four months ago, on September twenty-second, it's a Sunday night, he goes into the lab like usual and opens the freezer cabinet they got built into the wall. I haven't seen it so I can't be too clear on the specifics. Out comes Dr. Valentine.''

Tubby told Flowers how the doctor's head had come loose.

"That's a new twist," the detective said in admiration.

"Ain't it though," Tubby agreed. "A real turn of events. Busters says it wasn't him that twisted it though. He didn't touch it, even. Apparently to freeze a body hard enough for that to happen takes a couple of days. The coroner says Dr. Valentine had to be put in the closet no later than the previous Friday night.''

"Was he already dead when he was put inside?''

"Not sure. Dead or unconscious. He may have been stuck with something like an ice pick before he was frozen.''

"How did the police decide it was Busters?''

"He was the most available target, is what I think. But he was working Friday and had the opportunity. He seemed to be fleeing the scene when a security guard discovered him, in the lab, with the corpse. He has a drug prior. His fingerprints are on just about every drawer and cabinet in the place where drugs might be kept. The cops searched his house on Piety Street and found some bottles of pills from the medical center, and some other paraphernalia. And he had no business going into that freezer.''

"But no confession?" Flowers was writing fast.

"No. He denied everything. I've got to go see him at Parish Prison tomorrow. I haven't met him or heard his side of the story yet.''

"What do you want me to do?''

"First thing is get some background on Dr. Valentine. You know what to look for. Talk to his wife. The police report identifies one colleague by name, Randolph Swincter, M.D. He works in the same lab. See him. Find out what you can and report back.''

"How about your client? Should I check on him?''

"Not yet. I'll see what he has to say first.''

"You say your trial is in a week?'' Flowers said, meaning, "Did you screw something up, Tubby?''

Tubby didn't explain.

"Right,'' he said. "I'm going to throw myself on the mercy of the court and beg for more time. But you need to assume the worst. Jump in with both feet.''

"Geronimo!'' Flowers said, and vanished out the door.

Fast-moving for a big dude, Tubby thought to himself. Man, it sure was fun having a detective on the case. Now how the hell was he going to pay for him?

Now for phase two. He dialed the number for the *Times-Picayune*.

"Kathy Jeansonne, please.''

"Hello, Kathy,'' he said when he got the reporter on the line. "You remember the case about the doctor over at the New Orleans Medical School who got frozen to death?''

"Yeah, and beheaded,'' she said eagerly.

"Well, I just wanted to let you know I'm involved. . . .''

A good day, he reflected as he drove uptown. The Dubonnet name might soon be back on the front page. And Cherrylynn had accused him of letting his law practice slide. Feeling lucky, he decided to call up Jynx Margolis when he got home to see what she might be up to this time of night.

But she was so outraged when he told her that her ex-husband was dating Tubby's ex-wife that he wished he had gone straight to bed.

"That absolute bastard,'' she said, her voice full of venom. "It's just his way of getting back at me.''

"That's what I thought at first, Jynx,'' he replied, trying to soothe her, "but probably we have nothing to do with it. Probably they just met and they like each other.''

"Sure, and rats sing. You don't think Mattie may be

trying to hurt you just a wee little bit? Or make you a tad jealous?''

To be truthful, that angle hadn't occurred to him.

''I don't honestly know,'' he said. ''She would have to be awfully devious for that, not to mention still interested in me.'' Neither of which, come to think of it, did he find that hard to believe.

''You should tell her to watch out for herself,'' Jynx warned. ''Byron sometimes gets violent.''

''Yeah. You told me that. You painted him as a pretty coldhearted son of a bitch.''

''He was sweet when we got married,'' Jynx admitted, ''but he turned bad as I got older. He doesn't like wrinkles.''

''Mattie has a few.''

''That's one more reason to think he's just doing this to hurt you or me. His tastes run to early bloomers.''

''We'll see,'' Tubby said inanely.

''We sure will. I bet he would hit on anyone he thought you were dating, if he got the chance.''

''I can't believe he's that intent on getting back at you.''

''You can believe it, all right. He's like a lot of men. Mean, mean, mean!''

Tubby's thoughts of cocktails by candlelight evaporated.

''Gotta go, Jynx,'' he said. ''I'm due in court.''

''And I expect he'll be back sniffing around my house next,'' she was saying when he hung up.

Staring at the ceiling, Tubby reflected about how much women could complicate a man's life. Have a couple of drinks, go to work every day, watch the Saints on the weekend, maybe play a little tennis or catch some music at a club: that was the kind of fulfilling life a man could happily lead—unless he started getting involved with women. He went to the kitchen and got a bottle of beer from the refrigerator, even though he really wasn't thirsty for it. He put it away in two long swigs just to show that nobody could say anything to him. Although, of course, there was nobody else in the house.

chapter 8

Tubby was back at his desk early the next morning, gulping black coffee, plotting strategy, and eating an egg and biscuit he had picked up from The Pearl. It was one of the old places that hung on in the midst of all the glitz downtown.

He buzzed Cherrylynn on the intercom and asked her to call the jail and find out what the visiting hours were. She said there was a Miss DiMaggio outside, anxious to see him.

Oh? Who was that? Then it came back. The friend Monique had written to him about.

"Okay. Show her in."

His first impression when she came through the door was positive. Blond frizzy hair, young, maybe twenty-five, some meat on her bones and broad on top. She was not a great looker, but she met his eyes directly and had an honest face. Jeans and a red plaid shirt hung loosely on her large frame.

Her impression of him, when he arose to shake her hand, was less easy to gauge. A little cautious. He offered her a comfortable chair.

"You're a friend of Monique's?" he began.

"Yes. She and I work out at the same gym."

"Right. She told me she wanted to get into shape. Which

for Monique, of course, is totally unnecessary."

"Exercise feels good, even if you're not a blob," she said.

Tubby nodded in agreement and abandoned the attempt to remember the last time he had worked out. He waited for her to continue.

"She says you are a good 'business lawyer.' "

"Well, thanks for the compliment. It depends a lot on the kind of business you're in. Are you having a problem, Miss DiMaggio?"

"I think so. It's like a family situation. You see, my father and his brother, my Uncle Roger, had an oil company. I mean my Uncle Roger still does, but my father is dead."

"I'm sorry," Tubby murmured. He leaned back in his chair and crossed his hands over his stomach.

"Thank you. He died last June."

"What kind of oil company?"

"Not what you think of normally—not Texaco or Exxon or anything like that. They leased mineral rights and sold their leases to the big companies. Once or twice they did some wildcatting. The company controls lots of oil leases around Lafayette and in southern Mississippi. It's called Pot O' Gold."

"Optimistic name."

"Yeah. My daddy was a dreamer. And it made good money, too. But now all of it is going to Uncle Roger."

"That's the problem?"

"Yes." She crossed her legs and leaned forward to hand Tubby a document rolled up like a scroll. It had a rubber band around it which popped when he tried to take it off. He spread the paper out on his desk. It was an engraved stock certificate, and it had a gold foil seal pressed onto one corner.

"Stock certificate number three for one thousand shares of Pot O' Gold, Inc.," he read, "issued in the name of Albert E. DiMaggio. That's your father?" he asked.

"Yes. Now Uncle Roger says that certificate is no good. He says my daddy only owned ten percent of the company and he owns the rest. He's got a stock certificate for one thousand shares too. That's certificate number one. And there's another one in my father's name for one hundred shares. That's certificate number two. Uncle Roger says the hundred shares is all my father ever owned.''

"Then how does he explain this, certificate number three?'' Tubby waved his scroll.

"He just says it's not real. But see the signature of the secretary on this? That's Jeanne Theriot. She's dead now. She managed the office for twenty years at least. She wouldn't have signed it if it wasn't official.''

"Does your uncle say it was forged?''

"He probably would. He just shook his head when I showed him the certificate and said it was no good. Then he said something like, 'That was just something your father dreamed up when I was in Mexico that time.' ''

"How did you get the certificate?''

"It was in my daddy's safe deposit box at the bank. We opened it after he died.''

"And you showed it to your uncle?''

"Yes, but not for a couple of months. It came up at a family dinner we had, because Uncle Roger told me he just sold some leases for about two hundred thousand dollars, and the buyer wanted him and me to sign a paper saying exactly how much of the money we were entitled to. He told me that my share was twenty thousand. I said to him that I thought him and Dad were partners, and he said they were, but not fifty-fifty. Then he showed me the so-called corporate stock record book, which is like this black Bible covered in leather, and it showed only certificate number one and certificate number two. The certificate to my daddy for a thousand shares wasn't listed in there.''

"Let me sum this up,'' Tubby said. ''Your uncle claims you have a hundred shares and he has a thousand. You say you both have a thousand shares, even-Steven. Or maybe that you even have a hundred shares more than Uncle Roger.''

"Right.''

"Where's your dad's other certificate, the one for the extra hundred shares?"

"I have that, too. Do you want to see it?"

"Yes. I'd like to see all the documents you have. Corporate record books, whatever."

"Does that mean you'll take the case?"

"I'd be glad to. How did you leave things with your uncle?"

"We're not talking to each other. When you meet him you'll find out why. He's real overbearing. He can be quite obnoxious. He also has a lawyer. Do you know George Guyoz?"

"Yes," Tubby said shortly. George Guyoz was also overbearing and obnoxious. He and Tubby had tangled in the past on the Sandy Shandell case.

"I guess you should talk to him." Denise hesitated. "How much do you cost?" she asked.

"I generally charge by the hour. It's hard to estimate right now how complicated this might get. Usually for something like this I would take a substantial retainer, but because of the recommendation you came with I won't need that. What do you say I take this on a contingency?"

"Meaning?"

"Meaning I'll take a percentage of whatever I get for you above twenty thousand. Your uncle has already offered you twenty. I at least have to beat that. The usual percentage is one third. I'd take twenty-five percent. That way you don't have to pay by the hour, and if you don't win something, neither do I."

"What if you have to sue Uncle Roger?"

"I still get twenty-five percent, even if I have to go to the Supreme Court."

"That sounds fair."

"But listen, I still get twenty-five percent even if I can settle this with a phone call."

"I see—so it's a gamble."

"Yeah. For both of us. Why don't you go home and think about it. Talk to another lawyer if you like."

She considered that for a second.

"No. It sounds all right to me."

"Great." Tubby reached over the desk and shook her hand. Her grip made him wince. "So what do you do for a living?" he asked.

"I teach third grade at Audubon Elementary. And I also box."

"Did you say box?" Tubby asked in surprise.

"Yes, women's boxing. There are about six girls here in New Orleans doing it. And others who do it recreationally."

"You mean you fight in the ring?"

"Oh yes. I've had two bouts at Coconut Casino in Bay St. Louis."

Tubby's mind was stretching. "That's quite unusual," he said finally. "Do you win?"

"I usually do. My professional record is four and oh."

"Wow! Professional record, huh. Where can I see you box?"

"My next match is tomorrow night at the American Legion Hall in Marrero. I work out every day at Swan's Gym off Simon Bolivar."

"Maybe I can get there. I've got an emergency matter that is taking up most of my time for the next ten days or so, though."

"I'm sorry," she said, immediately contrite. "I know I shouldn't have just dropped in. I was in the building using the bank machine downstairs, and I decided to see if you could talk to me."

"No, that's fine," he reassured her. "I'm glad you did."

She got up and offered her hand again. He was more attentive to her biceps now, and yes, she certainly had some pretty good muscles. He walked with her to the door and watched her behind as she walked lightly down the hall to the elevators. She had balance and agility, but couldn't a woman hurt her bosoms or something in a boxing match? Couldn't she get her nose broken? Tubby wasn't able to quite sort it out in his mind. He'd really have to see this for himself.

chapter 9

Tubby presented himself to the fat deputy at the counter, which was protected by a chain-link screen that reached the ceiling. The fact that the guard was a woman didn't make it any less intimidating.

"Hello!" he called, to get her attention.

It took the deputy a minute to tear herself away from the *Sports Illustrated* she was reading and, with irritation, acknowledge Tubby.

"I'm here to see Cletus Busters. I'm his lawyer."

"Sign in," the jailer directed. Slowly and deliberately she looked up Busters in her roll book.

"They're at exercise," she reported. "It will take a few minutes to get him down. Have a seat."

There were a couple of plastic chairs along the far wall, and the floor was littered with gum wrappers. Gum wads clung to the legs of the chairs. The wall was covered with rules, hand-lettered in blue and red on a white-painted piece of plywood:

NO EMBRACING ALLOWED
VISITORS TO BE LIMITED TO
FORTY (40) MINUTES

NO PROFANITY OR LOUD TALKING
NO KISSING

And, of course:

NO CAMERAS, RECORDING DEVICES,
VIDEO, CONTRABAND, WEAPONS, GUNS,
KNIVES, NONPRESCRIPTION DRUGS, FOOD
ITEMS, COSMETICS, GIFTS

Is Vaseline okay? Tubby asked himself. How about con-
doms? Jails made him think bitter thoughts.

"You can go in and wait," the guard announced.
"They're bringing him down."

She pushed a switch that unlocked a steel-cased door
with a heavy thunk, and Tubby pulled it open with effort.

"Back there," the guard instructed.

It was a room, small enough to be cramped by the table
and two plastic chairs inside. There was a mayonnaise jar
top for an ashtray. The brick walls were painted brown and
were unadorned, except by painted-over cracks and pits that
could have been dug by fingernails.

This was the nice room, for use by attorneys and their
clients. Regular visitors, like wives, saw prisoners through
a metal mesh within earshot of uniformed guards.

He heard Busters approaching before he saw him. What
alerted him was the sequence of passwords and clanking
doors as the dungeon gave up its prisoner. Then the slim,
pinched-faced man, curly jet-black hair cut close, was
brought into the room by a gangling Mexican boy with a
mustache and a baggy black uniform.

"Call when you're ready," the deputy told Tubby, lock-
ing him in with the prisoner.

Busters was a skinny man. He wore the orange jumpsuit
the jail provided, and it hung on him like a napkin on a
knife. He checked his seat before he sat down, maybe inspecting it for gum. He took out a pack of Camels.

"Have you got a light?" he asked Tubby.

"No, sorry," Tubby said, patting his pockets.

''How'm I gonna light this?''

''I don't know. I guess you can't.''

''Maybe you could get a match from the corporal,'' Busters suggested.

''Forget the cigarette for a minute,'' Tubby said testily. ''My name is Tubby Dubonnet. Mickey O'Rourke has asked me to help represent you. Next time I come I'll bring matches. Right now we need to talk fast.''

''What's wrong with Mr. O'Rourke?''

''To tell the truth, he's drinking too much to defend you properly.''

''Sure enough? I thought something was wrong with him. The way he talked, seemed like he had no confidence. I haven't seen him but the one time.''

''Yeah, well, he has a problem.''

''Man, I'm the one with the problem.''

''You got that right.''

''What you gonna do for me?''

''Look, Mr. Busters, I'm like an emergency repairman. I'm going to try to get your trial postponed. If I can't do that, we're in deep shit. Right now, I'm assuming the worst. I have to find out a lot from you in a hurry.''

''I need a good lawyer, man. I ain't never heard of you.''

''What?'' Tubby demanded incredulously. ''You can have the best lawyer you can afford. Have you got any money, Cletus?'' There was no air in this place.

''I'm a janitor. What kind of money you think I make?''

''Maybe you got some money hidden away from selling pharmaceuticals.''

''What you mean, pharmaceuticals? What's that shit? I don't do none of that.''

''Then correct me if I'm misunderstanding you, Cletus. You have no money and, unlike O.J., you cannot afford the dream team of your choice. To me that means you're stuck with what you got—a pro bono lawyer.''

''What's pro bono?''

''Nobody pays me.''

''This ain't fair,'' Cletus argued sullenly.

''Bingo. But here's the good news. I am a pretty good

lawyer. At least when I'm motivated. So you just got lucky, 'cause right now I'm motivated.''

"I've never had any luck in this whole world."

Cletus glared at his hands. Looking around at the drab cracked walls, the naked light bulbs inside protective wire fixtures, the dirty ceiling, Tubby had to agree with Cletus.

"Let's see if we can make some luck," he said. "I can't deny you're in a bad place, Cletus, but you're not convicted yet. What do you say?"

"I say it sucks real bad. They're gonna fry me."

"Negative thinking, man, gets you nowhere. To start off, tell me something about yourself. Like where you grew up. Are you from New Orleans?"

"Yeah. Ninth Ward. Right on St. Claude Avenue."

"Did you go to high school?"

"McDonough Number 82. I graduated."

"That's good. Any college?"

"No. I've been hustling or working since I was seventeen."

"Okay. When did you start working at New Orleans Medical Center?"

"Three years ago. I'm a janitor."

"Right. What did you do before that?"

"Same thing. Marriott Hotel. Out at the airport. I've had some good jobs. I always worked."

"What were your good jobs?"

"I just told you about them, man."

"Oh. Okay, what about your prior drug bust?"

"That wasn't my fault. Somebody put some stuff in my apartment. I didn't even know it was there. The police were looking for this dude's girlfriend for something she did, and they thought she was staying with me. So they busted down the door and searched the place. I was the only one there. They found the stuff in the couch. I told them I didn't know anything about it, but they didn't believe me."

"You copped a plea?"

"Yeah. I pleaded guilty to possession with intent and got three years. I did one year, six months, and four days, and

I was on probation after that." Like lots of people who had done time, Cletus could count the days.

"No other arrests or priors?"

"I got in a fight and spent a night in Central Lockup."

"No other drug arrests?"

"No. I don't use drugs."

"How'd you find out about the medical school?"

"I was a temporary, like day jobs. I did all right and they made me a permanent."

"No trouble on the job?"

"No, I get along fine there. Except with Dr. Valentine."

"What was wrong with Valentine?"

"He had an attitude. He reported me if there was a tissue paper left in the can. He actually looked for dust and fingerprints."

"That's all?"

"He caught me what he said was playing with the rats one night and told my supervisor."

"Why were you playing with them?"

Cletus met Tubby's eyes. "I hate to see them little animals all caged up. They generally just kill them, you know."

"Really? Why?"

"It's their experiments. They give them diseases. Some got tumors on their heads, like in their mouths, and kind of a mange on their bodies. I hate to see it. It ain't my business, but I try to cheer them up sometimes."

"Did Valentine ever say anything to your face?"

"Maybe once or twice. I didn't hardly ever see him. I came in at seven o'clock at night. He was usually gone by then."

"What did he say?"

"He asked me why I didn't spray 409 on the counters, and I said I did. He asked me did I touch his rats, and I said no. He accused me of taking some medicine, and I said no I didn't, 'cause I didn't."

"What medicine?"

"I don't know. Some kind of barbiturates."

"And you didn't?"

"No."

"What was your job?"

"Mop, sweep, and clean."

"What happened on Sunday the twenty-second?"

"That's when I found him?"

"Yes."

"Nothing but that. I was doing my job. I open the door and out he comes. I didn't know what it was. It sure scared me to death. And when that head broke off I was nearly sick right on the man. I dream about it almost every night. Can you get something to help me sleep?"

"Maybe. Did you work on the Friday before?"

"Yeah, I works every Friday."

"Did you see Valentine then?"

"No. He must have been gone."

"Did you see him over the weekend?"

"No."

"On Sunday night when you went in, nothing was unusual?"

"Not a thing. Same ol' place."

"Why'd you open the freezer door?"

Cletus didn't answer right away. He looked angrily at his cigarette pack.

"I couldn't say," he grunted finally.

Outside in the fresh air, Tubby tried to make himself relax. The day was turning cold and cloudy. His client had told him nothing he found useful. Tubby was not even sure he believed that Cletus was innocent.

The man was secretive, angry, and unsociable—just the sort of person judges and juries loved to chew up, spit out, and ship to Angola. He followed the chain-link fence wrapped in razor wire to the courthouse, sidestepping a scavenger searching for beer cans in a trash barrel.

He was depressed. "I'm getting older," he told himself. Funny, when you're young you want each day to be better than the last. After you've traveled a few miles, you just wish each day could be as good.

chapter 10

The meeting with Judge Stifflemire did not go well. The judge was not happy to see these two particular lawyers in his chambers, though he was polite enough to direct them to sit in the plush leather chairs facing his desk. Mickey O'Rourke, dignified but a little unsteady, took the one by the potted ivy. He became physically smaller under the judge's stare.

A child's crayon drawings were thumbtacked to the bookshelf behind His Honor's head, but they did not make the judge appear any friendlier.

Tubby said, "Good morning, Judge," and sat.

The judge glowered at him, too.

"Let me guess, Mr. Dubonnet. You are going to assist counselor O'Rourke here and represent Cletus Busters."

"That's right, Judge. Sort of on an emergency basis. Mickey, why don't you explain the situation to the judge?"

Stifflemire held up his hand to stop O'Rourke from talking.

"I think I understand the situation very well. You, Mr. O'Rourke, say you are unprepared for trial. You are unable to handle the rigors of being a lawyer, you say. You have brought in another attorney to help you. And you want a continuance."

"That's close, Judge," O'Rourke began.

"And I'm going to deny your request," the judge ruled.

"Your Honor," Tubby said, "I don't think you know the whole story. Let me explain what's going on."

"All right. I'll be fair, Mr. Dubonnet. But please make it short."

"Okay, Judge. No beating around the bush. Mr. O'Rourke has a serious problem with alcohol. He's sick. He shouldn't have been appointed probably in the first place to represent Busters. But whatever, he's not up to the job. He's got the shakes half the time. He's probably got a pint in his briefcase right now. His mind is a blob of Jell-O, no offense, Mickey. He's going to embarrass everybody if he has to try this case."

"Okay, so now he's got you to help him," the judge said reasonably.

"Yes sir, and I need to prepare the case. I simply can't get ready by a week from Thursday."

"What do you suppose Mr. O'Rourke has been doing for the past four months?"

"Mainly drinking Scotch, Your Honor," O'Rourke said sadly.

"Mickey, I've had enough of this," Judge Stifflemire snapped. "You were the same way in law school. Always fucking off. Taking things easy. Winning the Werlitzer case was the worst thing that ever could have happened to you. It was too easy. A quadriplegic crushed by a piano falls right in your lap. You didn't have to break a sweat to win a million dollars for him. So now another sob story from you."

"Judge," Tubby broke in, "this is unfair. The issue is not whether Mickey O'Rourke is a perfect human being. It's whether Cletus Busters can get a fair trial. This is a capital case, Your Honor. I need to construct a defense."

"I don't buy it, Mr. Dubonnet. Mr. O'Rourke has had ample time to prepare his case. I can't allow lawyers to manipulate this court's docket. If I let him push off this trial I'll have no end of lawyers in here telling me their drinking problems, their drug problems, or how they're not getting along with their wives, or their husbands, for God's sake. No sir. It's not going to happen, Mickey. You graduated cum laude from Loyola. You're in good standing with the Bar Association. I expect to see you in court next week, with or without Mr. Dubonnet."

"Judge," O'Rourke pleaded. He held his hand out, palm down and flat, and Tubby and the judge watched it flutter.

Stifflemire shook his head. "That's all for this morning, counselors."

He opened a file on his desk and started reading, or pretending to. Court was recessed. Tubby and Mickey O'Rourke exchanged helpless looks. They got up and left.

The next stop was no better.

"I'm going for the death penalty," Assistant District Attorney Clayton Snedley said cheerfully.

He was an ex-priest, and he loved his job, it being easier to punish the guilty than it had been to forgive them. They were in the main hallway of the Criminal Courts Building, their voices echoing in a swirl of lawyers looking harried and common people looking lost.

"On what basis, Clayton?" Tubby asked, his voice full of scorn. "First violent felony charge. No murder for hire. No multiple killing. This is a plain vanilla murder, if it even was a murder."

"What do you mean, if? You think the guy committed suicide by freezing himself to death?"

"Maybe."

"Bullshit. Read the coroner's report."

"I don't have it."

Snedley raised his eyebrows in surprise.

"You better get cracking, son. Trial's around the bend. This was a murder, fearsome and foul. Especially atrocious, heinous, and cruel. That's why it's a death case."

"That's weak, Clayton. Freezing is slow and peaceful. Main thing, though, is you got the wrong guy."

"I've got his fingerprints on everything connected with the killing. He and the deceased frequently argued. Busters was stealing drugs. He got caught and killed the witness. I've got a solid case.''

"What would you give for a plea?"

Snedley looked thoughtful.

"I don't really need a plea. I've got him by the balls. Maybe, just to save the taxpayers the cost of trial, I'd consider life without parole if he'll plead guilty to murder one.''

"How about manslaughter," Tubby suggested. "That's tough enough for an innocent man.''

"Nuts," the DA said.

"He says he didn't do it.''

"Look at the evidence," Snedley said.

"When?" Tubby asked.

"File your discovery notice. Bring me a copy. I'll handle it on an expedited basis. No secrets here. You could see the whole damn file this afternoon.''

"Okay. Thanks, Clay.''

"See you in the circus," Clayton responded, and he was gone into the crowd.

Tubby walked down the steps outside to where O'Rourke was waiting.

"This is a fuckup," Tubby admitted.

Mickey didn't reply, but when they reached the sidewalk he told Tubby he had a stomachache and needed to go home to rest.

"Come by the office as soon as you feel better," Tubby said. "We need your help.''

"Sure, Tubby," Mickey said, making no commitments, and ambled off toward the bus stop.

Tubby hurried to his car. He had driven the Lincoln today because the red Spyder's canvas top leaked even in mild humidity, but now he was afraid some kid might be stealing his road car's hubcaps. It turned out his automobile was fine, but he had a parking ticket—another black mark on the day.

The sad truth was, he had to learn a lot about Dr. Valentine and Cletus Busters in eight days. Tubby deeply re-gretted that he had stirred up the newspapers about a case that could potentially be a disaster. Bad press, he did not need.

chapter 11

Denise DiMaggio tossed her gym bag onto the floor and paced distractedly around her small apartment, punching on the air conditioner, stowing some empty juice bottles under the sink, and checking out what the refrigerator had to offer. It always took her a long time to settle down after a workout, especially on a night when Baxter Sharpe was coming over.

Exercise, breaking a sweat, taking a pounding, got her so high that she could almost fly like a bird. The experience of showering down afterwards was for her what a hot fudge sundae was for other people—pleasure sensuous beyond description. But then there was usually nothing to do until bedtime except think about her lesson plan for the next day at school—as if there were a new and exciting way to teach the multiplication tables—or watch dumb television. And lately, Baxter, her coach, came over sometimes, but that did not exactly make her life any richer.

He filled some crazy void in her, but he did not give her joy.

She had dreams about winnning a championship, about feeling powerful and victorious, about dancing around the ring wearing bright silk, hands waving in the air, while the crowd roared.

The doorbell rang.

"Hiya, sweets," Baxter said loudly, when she let him in. He was about her height but much chunkier and broader. He worked out a lot and brown muscles bulged under his T-shirt.

He hugged her. "You were looking sharp today"—his favorite expression. Baxter's mustache nuzzled her ear. She always felt small in his embrace.

"I felt pretty good about it," she said, which for Denise was high praise.

"You let Carmella get to you a couple of times with her left, but you'll improve."

"Or she'll break my nose." Denise frowned. "Come in, why don't you sit down."

He landed on the couch, and she fixed them both a glass of spring water with a wedge of lime.

She sat beside him.

"I don't know if I'm making progress fast enough," she said.

Baxter took a sip from his glass and slung his arm over the back of the sofa, letting his fingers graze her shoulder.

"You're doing fine, Denise," he said. "You just need some more coaching, that's all. You've gotta develop that upper-body strength." He squeezed her bicep.

She flexed. He squeezed harder.

"You think I'll ever make it?"

"I know you'll make it, baby."

"I just want to win so badly," Denise said. She could hear the crowd cheering.

Baxter's hand had drifted down to her breast.

"There are things I want badly too," he whispered.

Denise never liked this part as much as she was supposed to. It wasn't as exciting as the adrenaline rush she got when her right hook connected and her opponent's head snapped back.

Baxter had both arms around her now. He nibbled her neck and moaned softly into her ear.

She liked the warm feeling, the obedient feeling.

"I've got to see more of you," he said gruffly. "Stand up."

She did as she was told.

"Now take off that shirt," he demanded.

She complied, and while she pulled it over her head he reached out and traced a circle around her navel with his fingertips.

She stripped off the rest of her clothes, in the order instructed, and twirled around naked, hands clenched in the air imitating victory.

"You ain't quite won yet." He grabbed her around the waist, and she thought her spine would crack when he pulled her on top of him.

He was rough, and did not even get out of his pants. His blunt fingertips left marks on her softest parts, but she was used to pain.

After he was finished she curled up on a chair and looked at him.

"I think it's time I had a key to your place," he said, staring above her head. "We're starting to develop a relationship."

chapter **12**

Cherrylynn had spent the previous afternoon carrying discovery pleadings around the courthouse, finding a judge to sign them, and serving them on the DA. She waited while copies were made of those portions of the state's files Snedley was willing to let the defense see; then she brought it all back to the office so that by Thursday morning Tubby could sit at his desk and begin to read.

He now had the police report, including the officer's transcripts of his interviewees. They were Josef Malouf, the security guard who found Busters holding the frozen head; Dr. Charles Auchinschloss, the chief of the lab; and a Dr. Randolph Swincter, who worked there too. Tubby had the coroner's report. He had copies of fingerprint cards, marked to show where they were lifted, and with a number on each which he interpreted as the number of points each had in common with the fingers of his client. The numbers ranged from 10 to 12, and that sounded discouraging. Then there was his client's statement. Tubby settled back to read.

Malouf, the security guard, worked from four p.m. till midnight every night but Wednesday and Thursday. The body had been discovered on Sunday, and had presumably been converted from a physician into a corpse on the previous Friday, but Malouf had no light to shed on anything else. He had a desk by the entrance to the wing of the hospital that was occupied by the Moskowitz lab. Only authorized personnel were permitted past him. They had to show a plastic ID card, but they didn't sign in. Almost every professional and most of the normal people who worked at the hospital had the requisite plastic pass.

People came and went all the time. The corridors usually thinned out after nine o'clock, and the guard would generally walk around the halls at that point looking for anything unusual. Other than doctors necking in the labs, or escaped rats or rabbits in the hallways, he never found anything unusual. Until one Sunday night when he opened the door to Lab 3 because he'd heard noises, and found a frozen corpse and a frightened Cletus Busters.

He didn't remember when he had last seen Dr. Valentine. He didn't remember who had been in the labs Friday, day or night. The usual crowd, he said.

Dr. Auchinschloss, forty-three-year-old Caucasian male, reported that Dr. Valentine had been a fine researcher and that there had never been a single murder in the lab before. The institution's purpose, simply stated, was to identify diseases and toxins that threatened or killed people and to develop cures and antidotes. He may have answered the question about what projects Dr. Valentine was working on, but the cop interviewing him was way under water and summed it up with "poison research." Valentine worked closely with Dr. Swincter on several projects. He could promise that Swincter and the other six doctors on the research staff would cooperate fully.

Dr. Randolph Swincter, thirty-five-year-old Caucasian male, was shocked by his colleague's death. The two had collaborated on numerous projects and published several journal articles during their three years together. He had last seen Valentine Friday morning when they were both busy putting mice into the centrifuge to see what was on their brains. Tubby figured the police interviewer must have gotten that wrong. Swincter had left the lab at two o'clock, spent a couple of hours at the hospital library, then gone home to watch TV and eat takeout pizza. Vegetarian.

As far as he knew, no one disliked Dr. Valentine. Except maybe Cletus Busters, maintenance man, who Valentine thought might monkey with the mice after hours. Swincter had heard rumors that Busters swiped drugs from the hospital. He discounted them because, "If true, the guy would have been fired."

The coroner's report was only partly intelligible to Tubby, but it did eliminate the possibilities of suicide and accidental death. Valentine had been killed swiftly by a knife or other sharp blade stuck directly into the back of his head, severing the spinal cord, possibly just a few minutes before he was crammed into the freezer closet. This helped to explain the head's separation from the body. No weapon had been found, but the coroner stated the obvious and speculated that it could have been a scalpel. He estimated that death had occurred, and the big chill had begun, between four and eleven o'clock on Friday night. Medical literature, it seemed, was limited on the means to tell how long a frozen person had been on ice, so he couldn't be more precise.

Tubby sighed. He stood up and went into the tiny kitchen to pour himself a cup of coffee.

"How's it looking, boss?" Cherrylynn asked when he passed her desk.

"Complicated," he replied.

He was getting a headache.

"Have you got any aspirin?" he asked her.

"Sure." She fished a bottle out of one of her desk drawers.

He thanked her and knocked them back with a swallow from his cup. "See if you can reach Flowers," he instructed. "Ask him to come here first chance he gets."

She reached for the phone. Tubby trod softly back to the office and sat down to read his client's statement. It was the typed transcript of a taped conversation, recorded at 3:12 a.m. on the night the body was found.

He read again the story of the discovery of the corpse. There was nothing new, except when Cletus said, "It fell right on me like a mummy coming out of a coffin,'' Tubby could feel some of his client's fear.

Cletus knew nothing about nothing. He was just cleaning up, like he did every night.

Stapled to this was the transcript of a second interview with Cletus. It had been made two hours later, at five a.m., at police headquarters. It began with Detective Ike Canteberry giving Cletus the Miranda warnings. Cletus said he didn't need a lawyer. He had done nothing wrong. Detective Canteberry repeated the warnings, and Cletus said the same and added that he didn't like lawyers. The policeman got him to sign a statement agreeing that he understood his rights. There was a copy of the statement attached to the transcript.

The questions now were a lot more probing.

"Tell me again what happened, when you opened the closet door."

"The man fell on me, like in a horror show. I jumped out of the way, and his head busted off on the floor."

"You touched the body?"

"I sure did. I picked up his head and tried to put it where it was supposed to be."

"Why did you do that?"

"I don't know."

"Why did you open the closet?"

"I don't know. To clean it, I guess."

"To clean it?"

"That's my job."

"Had you ever cleaned it before?"

"No."

"Did you see the sign that said 'Do Not Open. Authorized Personnel Only'?"

"I don't remember."

"You didn't know it was off limits?"

"No."

"Did you open any other cabinets or drawers when you were in there?"

"No, I didn't."

"Have you ever been arrested, Mr. Busters?"

"No."

"Ever been convicted of a crime?"

"No."

"I'm holding a rap sheet here for one Cletus Martavius Busters. Says you've been arrested twice for possession of a controlled substance. One was dismissed. You were found guilty of intent to distribute over one ounce of cocaine. You were sentenced to three years at hard labor at the Louisiana State Penitentiary. Then you were on probation. That was six years ago."

"So?"

"You just lied to me about it."

The transcript reflected "[No Answer]."

"Why did you lie about it?"

"I was set up. I didn't do nothing alleged."

"Nothing alleged, huh? Says here you did."

"[No Answer]."

"Do you still deal drugs?"

"No, I never did."

"Did you know that drugs were stored in the laboratories you cleaned?"

"No."

"You mind if we search your house?"

"You stay out of my house. I thought you wanted to talk about Dr. Valentine. What's all this drugs, drugs? That ain't got nothing to do with anything."

"Didn't Dr. Valentine accuse you of taking certain types of drugs from the lab?"

"He didn't know what he was talking about. He didn't like me."

"Why?"

" 'Cause I took pity on his rats. I hated to see them treated like he did. He thought I was feeding them stuff from the vending machines."

"Did you?"

"No. All I ever did was talk to them. Stupid stuff."

"How did he know that?"

"He came in and saw me doing it one night."

"Doing what?"

"Just playing with the little rat."

"You had one out of the cage?"

"He had got out of the cage all by hisself. I was just putting him back in."

"What did Valentine do?"

"He cursed me out and made a report."

"What happened?"

"Nothing. Personnel people told me to stay away from them mice."

"Did you?"

"Yes."

"No more trouble with Valentine?"

"No."

"Where were you Friday night?"

"Me? Working."

"You went into that lab?"

"Sure, I cleaned it."

"What time?"

"I don't know. Probably nine or ten o'clock."

"Did you see Dr. Valentine?"

"No."

"Anyone else?"

"Not in there."

"Where?"

"I seen that security guard sitting at his desk eating potato chips."

"Did you play with the rats that night?"

"No."

"Did you open any of the drawers?"

"No."

"How about the freezer closet?"

"No."

"Why not?"

"What you mean?"

"Why didn't you open it to clean it, if that's your job?"

"I guess I figured it was clean."

"You guess?"

"Yeah."

"I think you did see Dr. Valentine on Friday night."

"He wasn't there."

"I think you got in a fight with him."

"No way. Maybe I do want a lawyer."

"I think you stuck Valentine into that freezer."

"No way."

"What did you say about a lawyer?"

"I want one."

"Okay by me."

End of interview.

Flowers arrived, bustling as always. Cherrylynn tried to keep up with him, but he barely slowed down on his way to the inner office.

"What have you got?" Tubby asked without preamble.

"Hello to you," Flowers said. "Okay. I can fill you in on our Dr. Valentine. I've spoken with a few of the other M.D.'s who work in the lab, including a Dr. Swincter, and nosed around his neighborhood some."

"And?" Tubby leaned back in his chair. It creaked.

"Thirty-six years old. Highly regarded in his field. He's published quite a few articles on unpronounceable topics, and I'm getting copies made for you. Most of them seem to deal with strange ways people die. Most recently he's been investigating, with Dr. Swincter, the death of a woman who drove off the Highway 11 bridge into Lake Pontchartrain after suffering a heart attack for no apparent reason. Her condition looked much like an allergic reaction, but to what? It's the kind of mystery that makes forensic pathologists happy to get out of bed in the morning. This I got from the head of the lab, one Dr. Charles Auchinschloss, a/k/a 'the dean.'

"Valentine, according to the dean, was a workaholic—only a couple of years out of his fellowship. Now he's a hot shot scientist and a consultant to medical instrument companies. In other words, he was poor as a blues singer just a little while ago, but now he makes lots of money to pay off all his student loans. He teaches at the medical school. He's socially connected and rode in the Momus parade at Mardi Gras. He goes home to a very pretty wife in a condo in River Ridge. Her name, get this, is Ruby. She is a nurse, but in a different hospital. They met at a convention.''

"Kids?" Tubby asked.

"None. They've only been married for two years. She seems to have adjusted well to his demise. It's been four months, of course, but she displayed no outward signs of grief. Sort of nice-looking. I could almost believe she was coming on to me.''

"A dangerous thing to do."

"Aw." Flowers looked hurt.

"Any impression of Swincter or Auchinschloss?"

"Swincter is your basic medical nerd. Looks decent enough. Cleans his nails. Has a difficult time conversing about anything other than his work. And when he talks about that you can't understand him.

"Dr. Auchinschloss is the opposite. I mean, he can gossip just fine but doesn't seem too plugged into what is actually going on in his labs. He projects the absentminded professor. He did mention that Valentine was recently on the search committee that selected him as the new assistant dean at the medical school. I get the feeling it was a controversial job.''

"Find out who got the job and who didn't."

"Not bad, counselor. What else do you want me to do?"

"We need somebody else to hang this murder on, so keep digging around the hospital. Have you talked to his students?"

"Not yet, but I'm getting some names.''

"Okay. And we'd better find out about our client. Take a look at the police report." Tubby gave Flowers the rap sheet. "Let's see what the hell he's up to when he's not opening freezer doors.''

"I'll stay in touch," Flowers said.

"Please do," Tubby called to his back.

• • • •

Tubby paced around his office. Shocking that there should be so much duplicity and pain in such a beautiful city. Even in the middle of winter, when those ay-yuppers in Vermont were tunneling through the snow to get to their cows, green trees lined the avenues of New Orleans. Gulf breezes brought the fragrance of marsh grasses and satsuma trees. Mardi Gras balls and King Cake parties had begun. Seagulls sailed serenely over the riverbanks, rich with supper. If people could not live in peace here, where could they?

Tubby was daydreaming himself into the governor's mansion when the phone rang.

The invitation to dinner was quite unexpected.

"I'd like you to get to know him," Mattie explained.

"That's very thoughtful of you," Tubby said. "Don't forget I actually know Byron already, since I sued him and took his deposition twice. I don't really think he wants to have dinner with me."

"Of course he does," Mattie insisted. "It might be a little awkward, but I feel the need somehow to be able to sit down like adults and be sociable. You could bring some ladyfriend as your guest. It would be a foursome."

"Mattie. I don't want to do this. I'm not seeing anybody seriously right now. It would be too strange."

"Do it for me, Tubby. It's crazy, I know, but I can't seem to let myself be completely free with Byron until I somehow have your blessing. It would help me make a break."

"Jesus, Mattie, you have my blessing. Please be free." He thought he was going to gag.

"Tubby, it's a simple request."

"Oh, all right."

"Thank you," she gushed. "We'll go to the Steak Knife up in Lakeview. It will all be very nice and civilized. You bring some nice woman. I know you must know one."

Was that a barb?

"Okay," he said.

"A week from Friday night?"

"No."

"Sunday night."

"Okay."

"You're a sweet man."

Good God.

"Mattie, have you talked to Debbie lately?"

"You mean about her being pregnant?" she replied bluntly.

"Yes. I just didn't know if she had told you yet."

"Of course she told me. I'm her mother."

"What do you think?"

"I like Marcos a lot. I hope they have the baby."

"She's so young."

"You may be forgetting how young we were when we got married."

"I just hate to see her forced into growing up so fast."

"We all make our choices. And the circumstances were about the same for you and me, if you recall."

"Were we really so stupid?"

"I think they call it innocent. And you've always been the innocent one, Tubby. You don't ever know what's happening unless it hits you right in the face."

What was that supposed to mean?

chapter 13

The sidewalk outside of the New Orleans State University Medical School was, as they say in south Louisiana, hot faché. People waiting for the bus grabbed at bits of shade in desperation—wedging themselves into the shadows cast by a stop sign or a telephone pole—and tried to stand motionless with minimal mental activity. Praline vendors, panhandlers, doctors and nurses in white coats, all floated languidly, in a slow glide, through the bright shimmering air. But inside the hospital the weather was cold, brisk, and clean. Say what you will about the great American healthcare crisis, Tubby reflected as he took great gulps of air-conditioning, there was an awful lot of money moving through the hospital system.

An information lady dressed in a pink apron told him which colored line to follow to reach the Moskowitz Memorial Laboratory. It was not a short hike, on the narrow yellow trail, and the number of people in the halls thinned out considerably as he penetrated further into the healing maze.

At last the line disappeared under a set of swinging doors with an imposing sign on them that warned all but authorized personnel to go away.

Tubby forged ahead. The hallway continued, and he

passed side doors to what he thought must be laboratories. All were closed, and cartoons from magazines or home-made curtains covered up the glass observation panels. At a point where the hallway made a T, there was a desk and a chair and a sign that said SECURITY. No one was sitting at the desk, and Tubby searched the walls vainly for some clue to the whereabouts of Laboratory 3, which was where Cherrylynn had said he was to meet Dr. Swincter at noon.

A woman wearing a green shirt and baggy pants, with puffs of paper around her hair and shoes, shuffled around the corner.

"Can you tell me where Dr. Swincter's lab is?"

"At the end of the hall, the door on the right," she told him, without turning her head or slowing down.

The door to Lab 3 also had a sign on it that read: NO ADMITTANCE. AUTHORIZED PERSONNEL ONLY. There was a window maybe ten inches square at eye level, but it was covered from the inside with a piece of yellowing notebook paper.

It slid open suddenly and a slim man wearing a tan suit, looking self-assured and untroubled, stepped into the hall.

"Excuse me," "Pardon me," he and Tubby mumbled to each other while they did a clumsy dance; then the man walked swiftly away, leaving a breeze of cologne.

Purple Musk? Tubby guessed, remembering his daughters' birthday gifts, intended to improve him, neglected on his dresser at home.

He pushed the shiny handle tentatively and peeked around the edge of the door. He saw white walls, stacks of gray metal cages, and long counters topped with bright stainless steel. At the center counter, on a stool, a short man sat with his head in his hands.

"Pardon me," Tubby called, and stepped in through the doorway.

The man looked startled, as if not many people came in here, and Tubby saw a look of irritation cross a strained and very businesslike face.

"Yes?" the man said, raising one bushy black eyebrow in a manner designed to dismiss orderlies and civilians.

"Excuse me," Tubby said. "I'm looking for Dr. Swincter."

"That's me," the doctor said, and patted the pockets of his lab coat.

"Hi, I'm Tubby Dubonnet. You talked to my secretary."

"Oh, yes," the doctor said resentfully. "I have so little time . . ." he began, but he was distracted when the door behind him whooshed open again. A dark-haired woman, also wearing the standard white uniform of the hospital officer corps, entered the lab.

"Excuse me, Trina," Swincter said. "This man is the lawyer for the fellow who killed Whitney. I'll be a little while."

She looked Tubby over carefully as he offered her his hand.

"Trina Tessier," she said, and gave his fingers a quick touch. "Come to my office when you're finished," she told Swincter, and was on her way out the door. A bit of red skirt flew below her white coat, and there was a quick flash of pale ankle.

Tubby watched Swincter take in the view.

"Thanks for seeing me," he said, breaking the doctor's reverie.

"Oh, sure. I guess you're trying to get Cletus off."

"Well, I'm trying to find out what happened. Do you know Cletus well?"

"Seen him around." Dr. Swincter had a funny way of talking, like scissors neatly trimmed every word. And yet his soft lips barely moved. But his blue eyes jumped around the room. Tubby would have judged him to be more than forty-five years old had he not known him to be about a decade younger.

"And of course you knew Dr. Valentine."

"He and I worked together for almost three years."

"I don't know very much about what kind of work Dr. Valentine did. Some sort of research on disease prevention?"

Dr. Swincter looked like he was being confronted with a soda-slurping seven-year-old on a field trip.

"A little more complicated than that, actually. It has to do with isolating viruses or toxins, and developing medicines or antidotes to treat them."

"How is the research funded?"

"Why is that any of your business?"

"Gosh, Doctor, I don't know. I've got a man charged with murder who may be executed with an injection of an extremely deadly toxin unless I can cast doubt on his guilt. I'm starting with a clean slate—just looking for information. Have you got any reason to believe that Cletus Busters did it and that I'm just wasting my time?"

"The police arrested him, didn't they?"

"So what?"

"He stole drugs from the hospital. He was unbalanced. He tampered with our experiments."

"You mean he played with the mice." Tubby nodded at the wall of cages from which small rustling and scratching noises came.

"Yeah, he played with the mice, and probably touched them, exposing them to uncontrolled bacteria. He possibly fed them, jeopardizing the entire sample in some experiments and months of work."

"But why would he kill Dr. Valentine?"

"Maybe because he's a deranged, violent man. I don't know."

"Would you grant the possibility that someone else might have done it?"

"I suppose so, but I think it unlikely."

"Okay, but you're a scientist and you know that the truth often lies in unlikely places. Sometimes you find it by expanding your search."

"All right, Mr. Lawyer. Our funding comes from many sources. The National Institutes of Health, pharmaceutical companies, some private foundations, some from the hospital itself."

"What was Dr. Valentine working on at the time of his death?"

"Several things, like all of us. We were working together on a long-term research project involving the outbreak of

a new stomach-eating bacterium that struck several blackjack dealers in Las Vegas about a year ago and then disappeared. We're also testing a viral inhibitor that shows
some promise in the treatment of AIDS. And, of course,
we always have a couple of check-ins.''

"Check-ins?''

"Term of art. People dead and the coroner can't figure
out why. They're sent here to see if we can point the pin
to the cause of death. Never know, we might find a new
bubonic plague.'' He looked hopeful.

"Was Dr. Valentine looking at any check-ins at the time
of his death?''

"Yep.''

"Can you tell me about them?''

"In a general sense, sure. We had two, I think, when
Whitney was here. A woman who passed out driving on
Highway 11 with predictable results and a Texas turista
who flew in on Taco Airlines and died in a taxicab on her
way from the airport to Bourbon Street.''

"What was strange about those deaths?''

"The local woman was in the peak of health, fifty-two
years old, a young grandmother. No reason for her heart to
stop. She had systemic palpable petechial rash covering her
extremities. The tourist had erythematous bullae, red blis-
ters full of pus, to you, on her chest and stomach. The
medical examiner didn't want to touch her, even with
gloves on. Other than that, what can I say? They were both
female, both were having their periods, and they both died
for an unknown reason. That's our clientele.''

"Sounds interesting. What happened to all of his work?''

"I've taken it over as best I can. Dr. Tessier, whom you
just met, is covering some of it. We have been interviewing
some good people for the vacancy Dr. Valentine left.''

"Dr. Valentine also taught at the medical school?''

"Oh, yes, we all teach.''

"What were his subjects?''

"Forensics and virology.''

"How many students did he teach?''

"About twenty in each course. They are advanced seminars."

"Was he a good teacher?"

"That's not really relevant in medical school," Swincter said curtly. "We expect students to learn what's being taught. The teacher grades how well the students are doing their job."

"Sounds pretty stressful."

"That's the point. I guess law school is like a kindergarten version of that."

And you are a pompous butt-head, Tubby thought.

"Was Valentine well liked?" he asked.

"I suppose," Dr. Swincter said, as if it mattered.

"Did you know Dr. Valentine's wife?"

"Sure. Ruby. She's a survivor type. Won't stay down long."

"Were they happily married?"

"Can't say as I know. Look, I've got a class in just about three minutes."

"Okay. But as a scientist, can you think of any avenue of inquiry I'm overlooking?"

Swincter seemed intrigued. He smiled slightly, as if he was about to say something, but then he compressed his pink lips and said, "Nope."

"Thanks anyway," Tubby said. "You may see me or my people poking around over the next few days. Have you been asked to testify for the prosecution?"

The doctor frowned. "Yes, I have, though it will undoubtedly be very inconvenient."

"What did they ask you to testify about?"

"Catching your client playing with the mice, as you say."

"Is that what they are, in these cages?"

"Yes, come on, I'll show you."

He led Tubby across the lab to where shoebox-sized cages stacked a dozen high ran the length of a wall. Each had a plastic label on the door, and inside were white, furry creatures. Some you'd call mice, some rats, and some were hamsters or rabbits. The sides of the gray metal cages were solid so they couldn't see each other, but tiny pink noses wiggled through the screens of many of the hutches. The occupants made little squeaks and fluttering noises.

"Here's the farm," Dr. Swincter said fondly, a shepherd looking over his tiny flock by night.

"What do you do with them?"

"Basically we infect them. Some we dissect, and others we cure. We're a mean bunch of bastards, right?"

Tubby shrugged. He noticed the freezer cabinet across the room and studied it with fascination.

Dr. Swincter looked disappointed not to get more of a reaction.

"I thought Valentine found Cletus touching the animals. What exactly did you see?" Tubby asked.

"It was Valentine who caught him. He saw Cletus tampering with some white mice."

"Tampering?"

"He was sitting right behind you, according to poor Whitney. On the counter. He had a mouse in each hand, and he was petting them with his thumbs."

"How did that affect your experiment?"

"Well, for one thing, we didn't know which mouse was which. So we had to guess what cages they came from. And naturally the whole experiment was suspect since we didn't know how many others he might have been taking out and switching around. We had about forty subjects then."

"So then what did you do?"

"We had to burn them all and start over."

Tubby's stomach flopped over.

"Well, thanks for the interview, Doctor. I'll be going now. Have a good class."

Swincter appeared satisfied at having grossed out a lawyer. He shook Tubby's hand and turned to walk away.

"Doctor," Tubby said. Swincter looked back.

"Where do you keep the check-ins?"

"In the freezer, Mr. Dubonnet. Same place they found Dr. Valentine."

He turned again, and Tubby left. As he walked out he

noticed that there was now a guard at the security desk, a stocky Mediterranean-looking man with a policeman's hat and a "Medical Center Security" patch on his chest. He lifted one lazy eye and nodded to Tubby as he walked past.

chapter 14

Ever since their first "date" on Christmas Eve, Baxter had started showing up at Denise's apartment unexpectedly. She found it unsettling but wasn't sure what to do about it. He was her coach, and he was very physical.

"Hit me back," he commanded one time, and started sparring with her. He slapped her cheek so hard it made her eyes water.

She was so surprised that she reacted automatically and gave him a shot with her left fist that put a little blood on his lip.

"God damn!" he yelled, and he socked her in the gut with such force that she fell backwards onto the floor.

He pinned her there and entered her violently.

It was the first time she had ever hit a man, and she wondered what she could accomplish if she was prepared.

It wasn't always bad, of course. Sometimes Baxter really seemed to care.

He asked her once about how her day had gone, and she told him about a sweet note she had gotten from one of her third-graders and some other cute stories he seemed to listen to.

She told him about her dispute with her uncle over the family business, and about going to see a lawyer.

"Ever since my father died, Uncle Roger has been trying to force me out of the company. Mr. Dubonnet is trying to get me my shares back," she explained.

"You shouldn't fight in the family," Baxter said.

"What about your wife?" Denise asked.

"She ain't family," Baxter said scornfully. "She's just a bitch who tricked me into marrying her. Believe me, we don't have anything going anymore. As soon as I find the right lawyer I'm gonna get a divorce."

"What about my lawyer?"

"Yeah, I might call him. Has your uncle always been a shit?" he asked, getting back on safer ground.

Denise squirmed around in her chair. "I used to think he cared for me, but he turned out to be the biggest sicko I know."

"Why? What did he do?" Baxter inspected his forearm and flexed it to make the veins wriggle around.

"I don't like to talk about it. I think that's where all my problems come from."

"What problems have you got, babe?"

Denise stared at Baxter. His mustache twitched. One problem, she thought, is I'm always scared. Another is, I'm scared of you.

"I don't know," she said.

"I understand," he said, and he put his big arms around her.

She cried softly.

"That's my little girl," he crooned.

"We've got a real Melrose Place developing here," Flowers reported.

"What are you talking about?"

"Peyton Place for your generation, Tubby. Everybody's cheating on everybody. Ruby, the dear doctor's wife, is seeing a chiropractor."

"For what?"

"For romance. I saw her go to his home last night and not come out till the wee hours. One Ira Bennett. 'New

Age Chiropractic Clinic' on Prytania Street. And the deceased himself is mourned by at least one of his students.''

"He was dating a student?"

"Yeah, right. Dating. He was slipping around with twenty-six-year-old Magenta Reilly, second year. So says her former roommate who got fed up with the distractions in their apartment and moved out. Valentine was a lady-killer. Very full of himself. I gather Magenta wasn't his only girlfriend.''

"So Valentine is sleeping around. The wife is sleeping around. The husband is dead. Maybe you think this means there may be people beside Cletus with a motive to kill the good doctor.''

Flowers nodded affably.

"Have you talked to the chiropractor or the student?"

"No, and I haven't talked to Mrs. Valentine, either.''

"Okay. Let's make a plan.'' Tubby was going to enjoy this case in spite of himself. "I want you to go see the chiropractor. I'll see the wife. I think I'll see if maybe Cherrylynn wants to meet the young medical student. Could you show Cherrylynn where to find her?"

"Sure, she's mostly at the library, or in school, or at a bar behind the hospital called Mosco's where all the nurses and doctors hook up to get blitzed. But this is really hands-on stuff. I've never known you to want to get so involved in the, shall we say, fieldwork.''

"Take it as a sign of desperation. Have the police spoken to any of these people?"

"Just the wife, far as I know. The officer in charge is Fred Porknoy, who, you'll remember, isn't too helpful. The boyfriend and girlfriend are exclusive information, just for you.''

"Damn. Isn't Fred Porknoy the dope that Fox Lane said screwed up the Darryl Alvarez bust last year?'' Fox Lane was one policeman Tubby respected without reservation, even though Fox had had the poor judgment to attend law school.

"That's him.''

"Somehow they arrested Darryl for drug smuggling but

let the smugglers sail off down the bayou unmolested.''

"I remember.''

"Well, talk to the New Age chiropractor and see what you can develop. Then I suppose we could lay it all out for Porknoy and see if we detect a pulse. And I'll call Fox to see if there's a way to light a fire under these guys. We need help. There's no time for private citizens to be playing Paul Drake. Trial is in six days.''

"I've also learned a couple of things about your client.''

"Shoot.''

"Cletus Busters is believed to be respectable. Good family man until his wife left him. Pays his bills on time. Doesn't curse. Except perhaps in connection with his second job as a witch doctor . . .''

Tubby covered his face with his hands.

"Enlighten me,'' he groaned between his fingers.

"Yeah, he does voodoo cures and casts spells,'' said Flowers, enjoying himself. "He has a little shrine in the water heater shed behind his house. One of the neighbors had to put out a fire with a garden hose last year when Cletus went to Time Saver and forgot he had left some candles burning. Some leaves caught on fire, and it was pure luck the neighbor saw it or the house might have burned down. The neighbor says he popped open the shed door and there was a dead chicken on a blanket, some Mardi Gras beads around it, an unlit cigar on top, and a circle of candles.''

"We're all entitled to our personal eccentricities,'' Tubby said judiciously.

"Makes you wonder what he does with mice, though.''

"Ah, yes.''

"Or heads.''

"Jesus, that's right. What other good news do you have for me?''

"He's not known as a drug dealer. My guess is, whatever he may have taken from the lab was for his own use.''

"Or for his religious practices.''

"That, too.''

Cherrylynn announced that Kathy Jeansonne from the

Times-Picayune was on the phone requesting an interview.

Feeling the stress in the muscles of his neck, he reached for the telephone.

"How are you, Kathy?"

"Working on a deadline," she said. "What's the latest on the headless man?"

"Trial begins on Thursday. You may quote me as saying the police investigation has been superficial and shoddy. Without regard to other obvious suspects in the case they have focused on one black janitor. Why? Because he was available, and no one would complain. But now we are complaining, and I don't believe any fair-minded jury will convict Cletus Busters."

"Whew," Kathy said. "Keep it up."

"What they should do is convict the police department!" Tubby cried, outraged.

"Do you have any facts that will substantiate your statements?"

"We will present our case at trial," Tubby said ominously.

"Assistant District Attorney Clayton Snedley says he is going for the death penalty," Jeansonne urged.

"The time has come," Tubby declared, "when a jury in this parish will refuse to execute a man just because of the color of his skin and the emptiness of his pocketbook."

"Thanks a lot, counselor," Jeansonne said happily.

"Anytime," Tubby replied.

"Now if we only had a case," he said to Flowers, who was grinning at him in admiration.

chapter 15

Mourning doves nest in the eaves of the clay tile roofs of the Pontalba Apartments, the graceful red brick buildings that have faced each other across Jackson Square for one hundred and fifty years. Popular restaurants and shops for tourists occupy the sidewalk level. People with money who are attracted to nineteenth-century style, to ornate balconies, elegant dining rooms with tall ceilings and plaster medallions, and minuscule kitchens and baths, live on the two upper floors. A few are leased by corporations for the comfort of their clients and customers when they visit New Orleans.

Two men were drinking rum and tonic in a dim parlor. One was comfortably seated in a purple armchair beneath a portrait in oil of Judah P. Benjamin, the great Confederate, similarly posed. The other was reclining on a plush sofa facing him. Both were dressed for winter in the tropics: white linen pants, colorful shirts open at the collar, and Docksiders on their feet. The side bar was loaded with good whiskeys, setups, and ice. The French doors to the balcony were spread open, and the sounds and smells of the French Quarter floated in on the slow current of air stirred by the river.

"Walter, why don't you give me a report," the man in

the armchair, the older of the two, asked his companion.

Walter, looking debonair, sipped his drink. He had the soft brown eyes of a calf and a relaxed and carefree demeanor. He inclined his head so that it rested on the cushion and closed those dark eyes while he spoke.

"Busters's trial is next week. All the evidence points to him. It's in the bag. A new lawyer has been to see him. Some guy named Dubonnet, but he's not likely to do much more than ol' Mickey O'Rourke. It may even help because with O'Rourke drunk all the time the case didn't look completely fair."

"You don't consider this a problem then?"

"Probably not," the man on the couch replied, lazily running a hand through his hair. "O'Rourke is so out of it that the whole conviction might have been overturned on appeal. I'd say it's better in the long run to have another lawyer involved."

"Okay," the older man said. "Just so long as he doesn't get the man off."

"It won't happen," Walter said confidently. "The judge is holding firm on the trial date. This guy Dubonnet has been to see Dr. Swincter, but nothing strange about that. And he didn't learn anything useful."

"How do you know that?"

"Because I saw him there, and I made it a point to run into Swincter at the hospital yesterday morning, to show him our new laser line. I pumped him for everything that was said."

"Do you think it's such a good idea, Walter, being seen so much there now?"

"If anybody had asked, I was there on business, Mr. Flick. After all, selling medical supplies and drugs is my job. But nobody asked."

"Pharmaceuticals," Mr. Flick corrected automatically. With the fingers of one hand he brushed the knuckles of the other, as though petting himself. He had a thin face with skin soft as the leather of a good glove.

"I just don't want you seen anywhere near that lab."

"Of course not," Walter lied smoothly. "I talked to him

in the cafeteria." Walter regarded Flick as overly nervous.

"How is Dr. Swincter's research going?" Flick asked.

"Oh, his AIDS study is going great guns. All funding is secure. All of the other projects, however, appear to have died with Whitney Valentine."

"That's good. So far." Flick sipped his cocktail. "Is it your advice that we just sit back and wait?"

"I think we should keep a close eye on that woman, what's her name, Trina Tessier, who works in the lab," Walter suggested.

"Is she romantically involved with Dr. Swincter?" Flick asked. "I'm just curious."

"I'd like to find that out," Walter said.

"It's probably not important," Flick said. "But go ahead if you want. And you should keep monitoring these lawyers, Dubonnet and O'Rourke, from a distance, of course."

Walter nodded. Both men were silent for a minute, absorbing the pleasant noises of music and weekend merriment from Jackson Square.

"Would you like to stay the night?" Flick asked quietly.

"Why don't we go out for drinks and hear some music," Walter suggested. The sweet aroma of beignets drifted in from outside. "There's a great blues band, J. Monqué D, playing right down the street at Margaritaville."

"Maybe in a little while," Flick said. "The tourist attractions of New Orleans have never held that much interest for me."

"I know a more private club, if you like. It's all on the company, right?" Walter grinned. He had a silver case in his pants pocket, and he slid it out and worked his fingers around the engraving.

Flick didn't reply right away. Then he said, "I'd like it if you were to spend the night."

Walter swallowed what was left of his drink; then he put his head back and stared at the ceiling. He closed his eyes again.

Flick smiled and bent over smoothly to grab the bottle of Mount Gay from the butler's table.

• • •

Champs was a major hot spot for the young and restless. It was built over the water on Lake Pontchartrain near the yacht harbor. Guys with sailboats could tie up alongside the bar and try to entice young girls to sunbathe on deck and rock with the waves.

On a sunny Saturday, all the boats were out and customer traffic was brisk. With all the windows open, it was cool inside. Denise DiMaggio leaned over the bar and waved until she got the attention of Jimmy, the bartender.

"Is Monique here?" she asked.

"I saw her a few minutes ago," he yelled. "I think she's upstairs."

"I can go up?"

"Sure," Jimmy said. The upstairs was semiprivate. It was where the money went, and also a few select patrons. Denise didn't want to interrupt Monique if something personal was going on.

The stairs were beside the bar. At the top was a big room with couches that was available for special events, and down the hall, a locked office. Denise was going that way when she spotted Monique standing on the balcony looking out over the boats and the sailors.

"Hi," she called.

Monique turned around and beckoned.

"What are you doing out here all by yourself?" Denise asked.

"Absolutely nothing." Monique's eyes were half open, and she wore a relaxed smile. Denise figured she had been smoking something. They were getting to be pretty good friends, possibly because they were both independent and lonesome, but she had not learned all of Monique's tricks yet.

They sat on a cypress bench and put their feet up on the railing.

"I opened up this morning and ran the bar until three o'clock when Jimmy came in. I was also here until two o'clock last night," Monique reported.

"I thought since you owned the place you wouldn't have to put in so much time."

"If you ever own a business you'll learn how precious a day off is. I haven't had one for two months."

"But you're off now."

"I sure am. So I guess it's not so bad. Want a cranberry juice and vodka?" Monique had a plastic pitcher and a bucket of ice on the deck.

"Oh, I shouldn't. Well, maybe a tiny one."

Monique plopped a couple of ice cubes into a clear plastic cup and carefully added the main ingredients. Denise accepted it from her hand.

After a sip she continued. "I went to see your lawyer, Mr. Dubonnet."

"Yeah? How'd you like him?"

"Fine, I guess. As soon as I mentioned your name he was very friendly."

"Tubby is sweet. He really helped me with the paperwork on this place and with getting custody of Lisa."

"He seemed to know what he was talking about. But he has another big case that's taking up lots of his time right now."

"He'll get around to you," Monique said absently.

"Are you doing okay?" Denise asked.

"Me? Oh, I'm fine. Just tired. All I do is work, and in the evenings take care of Lisa. I don't have a social life, but it's okay. How's your love life going?"

"I'm still seeing Baxter," Denise said.

"Your trainer?"

"Yeah."

"And?"

"Nothing much. We go to movies. He's got an apartment, you know."

"I thought he was married."

"He is," Denise conceded, "but he's getting a divorce."

"Hmph," Monique grunted.

"I'm probably stupid to be going out with him."

"So why do you?"

"I don't know," Denise said crossly. "He understands me. Or so he says. Maybe he does."

"You sound confused."

"I am. Let's not talk about him."

"Okay."

They drank in silence. The sun started to set over the lake, shooting fiery orange streaks over the horizon.

"It's so peaceful out here," Denise said.

"It can be," Monique agreed. "Sometimes it makes you feel lonely though."

"Lonely can be peaceful," Denise said. "Being here makes me wonder how I ever got into boxing."

"Because you're competitive, fast, strong, and aggressive," Monique suggested.

"But dumb, maybe," Denise said.

"That can get old," Monique remarked.

"I'm sure getting tired of it."

chapter 16

It was fun getting up early on Saturday morning and wait-ing for Flowers. Otherwise, Cherrylynn knew she would just sleep late and then probably do her laundry or some-thing. She was ready for action, carefully decked out in casual white shorts, sandals, and a purple passion top. She had gone out last night and bought it just so she could look nonchalant for the occasion.

Flowers rang the bell at nine o'clock sharp. She had de-cided to wear her brownish-blond hair up to show off her neck, and he complimented her on it after she ran down the stairs to open the door.

He looked good too, as always, tan muscular arms, brown slacks with a pleat, and hair combed straight back. She jumped into his new black Honda while he held the door for her.

Some classical music she could not identify was playing softly on the radio, and she liked that touch extremely well.

She gave him a big smile when he got in beside her. "Where are we going?" she asked.

"This is known as a stakeout, Cherrylynn," Flowers said, pulling away from the curb. "And detectives never know what they'll find when they're on a stakeout."

"Oooh, it sounds thrilling."

"I wouldn't expect too many thrills from Magenta Reilly. Medical students live really boring lives."

"Are we just going to watch her house?"

"Yeah, her apartment. We can see where she goes when she comes out and figure out how to introduce you to her."

"What if she doesn't come out?"

"Then you'll just have to knock on her door and barge right in. Today is our day to find out what Magenta has to say. We don't have the time to be too tricky."

"I've never really done this before. This is actually the first time Mr. Dubonnet has asked me to get involved in a case like this."

"I'm so surprised," Flowers said, and smiled sweetly at her.

"You can tell?" she asked.

"I had a hunch." He laughed. "But it shows he must trust you."

"Oh, he does. I'm a very trustworthy person."

"You're just not experienced as a detective."

"Right."

"Well, you have to be an actor, too. And you have to be able to act natural at whatever you're doing. If that fails, all you can do is fall back on the truth—introduce yourself as a private investigator and try to get whatever information you can. That may be the best thing for you to do anyway, since you don't look very devious."

"You don't know. I might be extremely devious." She was offended.

"Okay. Here's your chance to find out."

He parked under a Japanese magnolia tree, splendid in pink-and-white blossoms, and pointed to the house where Magenta Reilly rented an upstairs apartment. It was on a quiet street of nearly identical two-story homes near Jeff Davis Parkway.

"She lives upstairs. The landlord is downstairs. She spent the night here, and we can afford to wait about an hour to see if she comes out into the daylight."

"Maybe she sleeps late on Saturday."

"Could be, but she answered the phone half an hour ago

when I called. She could have gone back to sleep, of
course."

"What did you say?"

" 'Wrong number,' and I hung up."

"How did you ever get to be a detective?"

"I went into the FBI out of college. When I left the
Bureau I didn't want to work for a living so I started doing
little jobs for lawyers and some insurance company investigators I knew. It grew from there."

"Why did you get out of the FBI?"

"I didn't like wearing a tie to work. It's a long story."

"We've got some time. You could tell me."

"No we don't. There's Magenta."

A small woman—the word "mousy" popped into Cherrylynn's mind—stumbled out the front door trying to hold
on to a blue duffel bag while extracting her house key from
the lock. She got herself organized and started off down
the street with her load.

"Laundry day," Cherrylynn said with resignation.

When Magenta turned the corner, Flowers started the car
and followed.

In the next block she went into a Naborhud laundromat,
and Flowers parked across the street.

"You sure you want to try this?" he asked.

"I can't back out now. Wait for me?" she asked, jump-
ing out.

"Sure, I'll be here."

That sounded good to Cherrylynn.

Magenta was pouring Tide into one of the washers. The
place was pretty crowded. A few students in cut-offs and
a bunch of Spanish ladies with round brown babies washed
and watched. The machines sloshed and spun.

Taking a deep breath, Cherrylynn walked directly to the
machine next to Magenta's and opened the lid, hoping the
owner of the clothes was nowhere nearby. The barrel of
socks and jeans gurgled to a stop.

She turned to Magenta. "Excuse me, are you a doctor?"
she asked.

Her question startled the young woman, but she said, "I'm a medical student. Why do you ask?"

"I just noticed all of your hospital kind of clothes. I'm thinking about applying to medical school, and I guess I wonder if it'll be the right thing to do."

"It's a lot of work," Magenta said, folding her empty duffel bag and putting it on top of her washer. "Are you in school around here now?"

"Yes, I'm a senior at Loyola majoring in biology," Cherrylynn said. Gee, lying was easy. "Look, would you have time for a cup of coffee or something while your clothes are washing? I'm really unsure about what to do. It would be a big help."

"I had planned to read this." Magenta showed Cherrylynn a textbook entitled *Cope's Examination of the Abdomen*. "But I guess a break won't really hurt."

"Thanks," Cherrylynn said. "There's a PJ's right around the corner."

They left the laundromat together, Cherrylynn chattering away about her imaginary life in college. She saw Flowers in his car.

"Excuse me just a second," she said. "That's my boyfriend over there."

Magenta watched Cherrylynn run across the street. Flowers rolled down his window.

"Everything's under control," she told him excitedly. "We're going to have coffee. You can leave."

"I'll call you later," he said.

"Lunch sounds good," she replied, and ran back across the street.

"He's cute," Magenta told her.

"He's a doll," Cherrylynn said. "He was coming to see if I needed help with my clothes, but I told him I'd rather talk to you while I had the chance."

Flowers saw them disappear into the coffeehouse and drove off in search of Dr. Bennett, wondering what a New Age chiropractor did on his day off.

•   •   •

While his troops were at work, Tubby got the word from his middle child, Christine, that Harold, his ex-wife's bum brother, was back in town. Tubby felt that one of his major accomplishments of the past year had been to arrange Harold's permanent departure from New Orleans. News of his return was all bad.

"He's staying with me—I mean at Debbie's apartment—for the time being," Christine told him over the phone. "I just thought you should know."

"Yeah, but what do you mean, 'with you'? You're not living at home?" He was referring to his ex-wife's home, which he had paid for. But so what.

"Oh, I've just been using Debbie's apartment to study in, you know, to hang out," she said vaguely.

"Where the heck is Debbie living?" he asked, showing some strain.

"She's hardly ever there, Daddy. Don't you know about her and Marcos?"

"Sure I know about them." Moving on. "But why are you hanging around her apartment? You need to be concentrating on your grades. College is next year, don't forget."

"My grades are fine, Daddy. We were talking about Harold. He's sleeping on Debbie's couch."

"Of course. Where else would he stay?" Tubby spat out rhetorically. "It would never occur to him to get a job or do anything else but mooch off his family."

"He's really down and out, Daddy. You should see him. He looks terrible. The way he stays inside the house all day, it's like he's afraid of the light."

"He's hiding from someone most likely. Is he doing drugs?"

"I haven't seen any, but I'm not there much during the day."

Tubby took that pitch.

"I should come over there and kick that little brat's butt," he said.

"Oh, Daddy." She laughed. "I do wish you would come

over and talk to him, though. Maybe you can find out what's really bothering him.''

Tubby was experiencing hot flashes.

"I'll come talk to him, all right. When is he there?''

"All the time, I think. He just watches television.''

"At least he's improving his mind.''

"He can be nice sometimes.''

Oh God, Tubby thought.

Lunch was not romantic. Tubby hailed Flowers on his car phone right before noon and asked him to collect Cherrylynn and report in. The conversation immediately turned to what restaurant they could eat at, and they decided to converge at O'Henry's by the river, where they could get a burger and munch peanuts.

As it turned out, Flowers and Cherrylynn in his Honda and Tubby in his Monza Spyder arrived at the same time and parked side by side in front of Yvonne LaFleur's, where creamy models attired in lace and white bonnets advertised Old South fashions to sugar daddies and debutantes. They strolled together back to Carrollton and noticed that, for some strange reason, there was no line outside the Camellia Grill, so they went there instead.

Tubby sighed in appreciation of the cloth napkins at the venerable diner shadowed by the avenue's towering royal palms. He signaled for coffee just to watch the graying black waiter pour a steady sable stream from two feet above the cup. Not a drop did he splash. Pleased with his stunt, the man gave Cherrylynn a kindly wink.

"Coffee or tea, ma'am?'' he asked.

"Tea,'' she giggled.

"Where's Harry?'' Tubby asked, referring to the waiter who had been a fixture in the place since Tubby was in law school.

"Harry retired,'' the waiter reported, ''after forty-six years. We got a sandwich on the menu named in his honor.''

"I'll have that,'' Tubby said.

Cherrylynn ordered a turkey club, Flowers the Doc Brinker's special double cheeseburger on rye, very rare, and a chocolate freeze.

The streetcar rumbled by outside.

"I guess we need to work," Tubby said grudgingly. "What happened to you?" he asked Flowers.

"I dropped Cherrylynn off with Magenta Reilly, Dr. Valentine's favorite student. Then I called on Ira Bennett, chiropractor. Who do you want to hear from first?"

"Cherrylynn, since she's the new kid on the block."

"Okay. Here I go." Cherrylynn told how she had gone into the laundromat on Tonti Street, how she had met Magenta by pretending to notice her hospital clothes, and how they had gone next door for a cup of coffee.

"I kind of worked around the subject of how hard medical school was and how it left so little time for a real life. I asked her right out if she ever had a chance to go out on dates. She almost started to cry, the poor thing. What she said was, 'No, there's never any time. You just have to realize that that part of your life is totally over.' I asked if she meant that it was on hold, instead of over, but she just looked real sad."

"That's it?"

"Pretty much. She told me she studied diseases because she wanted to make the world a more livable place. It seems she grew up in the projects and wants to, like, help people."

"I gather it was not your impression that she killed the doctor?"

"Not at all." Cherrylynn looked shocked. "She's real nice. And she seemed too sad and, well, meek."

"Okay."

"I do remember one other thing," she said.

Flowers and Tubby waited.

"She said she's learned that doctors are almost all assholes."

"A sweeping statement," Tubby murmured.

"No argument from me," Flowers said.

Their food came. The sandwich named for Harry turned

out to be roast beef on a seeded roll with melted Swiss and grilled onions covered with mushroom sauce. Tubby showed it to everyone to make them envious.

"So what have you got?" he asked Flowers.

"I've got a scrawny, bearded, slick-talking slimeball. That's my initial unbiased impression. His office is uptown on Prytania Street. He advertises himself as a chiropractor for professionals. I don't think he's doing so good because there was no one in his waiting room. His receptionist told me there had been a cancellation, so the doctor could make an exception and see me without an appointment. I had to sit in an examining room and wait for fifteen minutes. You know, they've got this strange chart of the human anatomy, according to the science of chiropractic, that shows how we've really got only one single great big nerve running through our entire body. Can you believe that? When Bennett came in I introduced myself and told him what case I'm working on."

"What reaction?"

"He pretended not to know what I was talking about and took offense that I wasn't there to have my spine adjusted. So I tried the direct approach and told him I'd heard he was having an affair with the widow Valentine. He got very huffy and asked how dare I insinuate such a thing. Basically he blew a fuse and ordered me out of his office, so I went peacefully."

Tubby chewed his sandwich thoughtfully. There was some garlic in there somewhere. "Good," he remarked. "I mean, it's good we're making our presence known. What time was it when you left Bennett's office?"

"Let's see." Flowers consulted a little notebook he kept in his pocket. "Twenty minutes past eleven," he reported.

"That probably explains what happened to me. Mrs. Valentine agreed to see me for a few minutes at her house. She's nice-looking, as you said, but kind of plump. She sat me down in the kitchen and fixed me coffee. I told her how sorry I was about her terrible loss and explained I'm just searching for another possible explanation of her husband's murder—one that doesn't point a finger at my client.

"She said she understood that this is my job, but she knows no one who disliked her husband. He never complained about anyone at work, or at the medical school, or anywhere else. They were extremely happy and hadn't a care in the world.

"Then the telephone rang and she took it there in the kitchen. When she came back she told me forcefully that she had spent as much time talking to me as she was going to. I also went peacefully."

"So now we have two great suspects who won't talk to us," Flowers commented.

"What does it all add up to, Mr. D?" Cherrylynn asked.

"Not a big hill of red beans."

A crowd had built up outside the restaurant. People loved the place, just because it served big portions of real food and was clean. A child outside, nose pressed to the window, watched the three of them sitting there. Please get up, those eyes said, so I can come inside for a piece of pie.

"Let's go," Tubby said.

He paid at the register and followed his two investigators outside. The waiting crowd parted, happy to see them leave.

"Cherrylynn, you can go to the office now, or in the morning," Tubby said, "but I want you to draw up subpoenas for all three of them, Ruby Valentine, the slimy Dr. Bennett, and your buddy Magenta. Get the sheriff to serve them first thing Monday morning. And I also want you to subpoena Auchinschloss, the head of the laboratory. And Dr. Randolph Swincter, Valentine's colleague, and anybody else I think of between now and then."

"What do you want *me* to do?" Flowers asked.

"Just keep a watch on Bennett and Mrs. Valentine. And see if you can think of any way to lay off some of your expenses on another client."

"Understood," Flowers said. "Where can I reach you?"

"Actually, that may be hard. I'm going to visit Busters again and then probably just go fishing and think about the problem." And about that damn Harold. And about Debbie. "Cherrylynn can take messages."

His secretary just shook her head.

chapter 17

Cletus Busters was a little happier on the second visit because Tubby brought him a pack of Camels and a lighter.

He lit up immediately and, between long puffs, asked Tubby how the case was coming. Tubby told him what they had done and whom they had talked to.

"Doesn't sound like much," was Busters's comment.

Tubby ignored him. "Were you working the Friday before you found Valentine's body?" he asked.

"I work every night but Saturday," Busters said, blowing a thin stream of smoke past Tubby's right ear.

"The coroner believes that Dr. Valentine's body had to be put into the freezer on Friday, or even earlier in the week, to freeze as solid as it did."

"So what you want to know?"

"First, did you see anything unusual on Friday, or earlier in the week?"

"No."

"Think about it. Can you remember anything on that Friday?"

"Not especially."

"Work backwards in your mind from the Sunday night you found the body. Can you remember what you did Sunday during the day, before you went to work?''

''Yes.'' But Cletus didn't offer to say what he could recall.

After letting the pause linger, Tubby prompted him further.

''How about the Saturday before you found the body, and the Friday before that?''

''It don't come to mind. One day's just like another.''

''Did you see anybody else in the laboratory when you were working?''

''Maybe one of the other doctors, like Dr. Tessier. They is there sometimes on a weeknight. You don't ever see them in there on a Sunday.''

''Did you see one of them on the night before your arrest?''

''No.''

This was a waste of time.

''The police found some drugs, some barbiturates, at your house. They came from the hospital.''

''So?''

''Come on, Cletus. It would help if you would open up to your lawyer just a little bit.''

''Do they say I took that stuff from the hospital?''

''Yes sir,'' Tubby said patiently. ''That's exactly what they say. What do you say?''

''They planted it.'' Cletus rocked back and forth and sucked deeply on his Camel.

Tubby just stared at him.

''Tell me about the cures you do for people.''

''Say what?'' Cletus's chair came back down to the floor with a loud clank.

''You know, the ritual services you do. Are they for healing people or, like, to cast spells? Come on, tell me.''

Cletus looked at him in disbelief. Tubby thought he was going to get up and leave.

''Who you been talking to?'' he demanded.

''Your neighbors, for Christ's sake, Cletus. What is it with you? You don't care if they kill you? Do you have some foolproof escape planned? Is that the reason you won't talk to me?''

"I don't like people getting into my business," Cletus shouted.

Outside the window, the guard showed his face. Tubby waved him away.

"Isn't that kind of a free-world luxury? You're in jail, and they tell you when to eat, sleep, and take a crap. They know what chemicals are in your urine. You're in danger of being strapped to a hospital gurney and getting an IV needle full of sandman drops stuck right up your business. It takes about a minute for it to work before your brain shuts off, and you can take your secrets into the nex world with you.''

"I don't fear the grave.''

"Then I won't feel so bad about losing your case, but it's a shame, don't you think, to let somebody get away with murdering Dr. Valentine?''

Busters lit another cigarette and thought things over.

"I'd rather die some other way,'' he conceded.

"Sure you would," Tubby encouraged him.

"I have powers that was taught to me. I can cure people and tell you what fork in the road will lead you where you want to go. I can also help you with your love problems.''

"All right. People pay you for that?''

"Some do.''

"Did you take drugs from the hospital?''

"Maybe a few.''

"Why?''

"To use in a ceremony.''

"Do you ever use body parts in a ceremony?''

"What you mean?''

"Like a head?''

"I never had no head to use.''

"Well, excuse me, but you were caught holding one.''

Cletus had no comment.

"Did you use mice or animals from the labs?'' Tubby resumed.

"I never troubled the mice but to play with them.''

"You don't use animals in your ceremonies?"

"Sometimes I might, but it's very rare. And I don't torture 'em none. They go quiet and quick. You want to see animals suffer, go see those with the sores and infections at that Moskowitz lab. You'll see plenty of 'em like that there."

"You disapproved of that?"

"I don't like it."

"Did you argue with Dr. Valentine about it?"

"He might've argued. I didn't."

"Did you kill him?"

"No, I didn't."

"Did you put him in the freezer?"

"Course not."

"Why'd you open that door up?"

"To look at the bodies or whatever they had in there."

"What the hell for?"

"I get a lot of my understanding of nature and power from what I see. I was studying."

"You don't know how Dr. Valentine got into the freezer?"

The sound of gospel music on the radio drifted up from the cell blocks. It was very mournful.

"No."

"You don't have any idea who put him in there?"

"No."

"Do you like white people in general, Cletus?"

Busters smiled with his lips, but Tubby wasn't sure about his eyes.

"Not generally, no. Some is probably all right."

"You weren't casting spells on Dr. Valentine."

"Not any big ones."

"How about on the other doctors?"

"They never bothered me except that Swink or whatever his name is."

"If you can tell people what fork in the road to take, why can't you see into space and tell me who killed Dr. Valentine?"

"I ain't tried."

"Well, as a favor to me, now that we've had this little talk, why not try?"

"It'd be hard to do in here."

"There's nothing easy in lockup, Cletus, especially opening the lock, but that's what you've got to do."

Tubby left Cletus Busters to commune with his spirits. It was, as always, an enormous relief to step outside into the littered, cluttered, loud, and busy free world and get away from doors that clanked when they closed. It was no easier out here to find the right fork in the road, but at least if you happened to stumble on it, you could take it.

chapter 18

The two boxers danced lightly around the ring and then slammed into each other in a flurry of elbows and fists. Stung, they stepped apart and danced some more. They wore fat red gloves and sparring helmets as a concession to safety and brightly colored shorts, one lavender and the other yellow. Pink tassels flew from their high-top shoes. What was unusual was that they were not bare-chested, like your regular, sweaty prizefighters, but wore vinyl pads on top that laced up the back. And they had long hair escaping from beneath their helmets.

Again the sudden collision of arms and gloves, and one of the girls sprawled head over heels onto the mat. She shook her head to clear it and jumped back up. A cut was bleeding over her left eye.

The coach was in the ring waving his arms.

"Too rough for sparring," he said, getting between them. "The idea is to work and learn, in and out, dodge the punch, not to hurt anybody. Here, Denise," he said to the one who had done the socking, pushing her back toward a corner. "You keep your left out further, all the time, like this. Don't let her get so close to you."

He turned back to the other woman, the one with the cut.

"You okay, Carmella? Nothing too serious, is it?" He

wrapped an arm over her shoulder and walked her over to the corner away from Denise. "That looked good, the way you jumped back up. That shows it was just a lucky fluke. All right, everybody, take a break. Hit the bag. Nobody gets hurt here unless they're getting paid."

Tubby recognized one of the boxers as Denise Di-Maggio, the woman who had come to his office. She had walked over to a portable cooler and was pouring water into a paper Kentwood cup. She was breathing hard and sweaty, but Tubby thought she smelled pleasantly like mushrooms on a good steak with maybe a vodka tonic to sip.

"Hi, Denise," he said.

She turned and looked him over.

"Mr. Dubonnet, you look like my high school principal in here."

"Well, gee, that really deflates a guy."

"Oh, I'm sorry. It's just the way you're dressed."

Tubby looked down at his gray suit, red tie with pictures of an endangered species printed on it, hard-soled, polished, wing-tip shoes. Then he pulled his stomach in. "I had to go to the jail to see somebody," he said. "They want lawyers to look like this, even though it's Sunday. You look different too. A lot more physical than at my office."

"This is what I'm doing every chance I get. Meet my coach."

Tubby looked around to find a bald young man wearing a tight black T-shirt over lots of shoulders coming toward them.

"Coach, this is my lawyer, Mr. Dubonnet. And this is Coach Baxter Sharpe."

"Nice to meet you." He studied Tubby suspiciously.

"You also take divorce cases, don't you, Mr. D?" Denise asked pointedly.

"Sometimes," Tubby said.

"Well, Coach Sharpe has a problem he might like to talk to you about."

"Yeah, sure," the coach said, "but I'm kind of busy right now."

"Here's my card anyway, Mr. Sharpe," Tubby said. "Give me a call anytime."

"I'll do that," Sharpe promised, and retreated toward the ring.

Denise led her lawyer away.

"I hope you didn't mind," she said. "I know you must get referrals all the time."

"I don't mind at all." Praise the Lord.

"I'm kind of excited you came down here. We don't get many spectators. I mean, ones we want."

"It's a first for me. Don't you get hurt?"

"Sometimes. Not very feminine, huh?"

"Sure it's feminine. Well, no, I guess I don't think of it exactly as feminine. It's not like I'm stuck on the weaker-sex thing. My girls, when they were little, beat on each other plenty of times. Heck no, it's probably good exercise for you."

She laughed at his confusion.

"It really is good exercise," she said. "Most of us get into this as part of our overall training program. And most of us work with Coach Sharpe. The money part of it is just now starting to happen."

"Is there a recognized league or something?"

"They're just beginning to get that organized. It's gonna be great. Right now we gotta wear these chest protectors." Tubby followed the pointed finger to her chest. "It's really uncomfortable."

"You'd, uh, prefer to box without it?"

"Absolutely. An Ace bandage or any good sports bra would be fine with me. I'm not built too big anyway." She laughed again.

"I'd say you're plenty big," Tubby said, and reddened. "I mean, I wouldn't want to get in a fight with you. What's the motivation? Money?"

"Partly, sure. But I like to be good at things, and this is something I'm good at. I like winning, too."

"Then you got a perfect spectator attraction here. It's fascinating to watch because you're certainly not brutes. Everybody's gotta be curious, however, why a pretty and intelligent woman would slug it out with another woman.''

"People think it's strange, that's for sure. But you know, that's not really my goal."

"What is?"

"Slugging it out with a man would be more like it."

"In the ring, you mean?"

"Sure. There's no reason why women and men can't compete in boxing so long as they're in the same weight class."

"Okay. That sounds more natural to me in a way than two women fighting. I suppose a man and a woman in the ring is like making some sort of statement for equality. Two women, to me, is more like something you can see on Bourbon Street."

"You're thinking about mud wrestling." She was offended by the comparison.

"I'm sorry," he said, backpedaling quickly. "I know this is really quite different. Anyhow, I'm over the shock now. I'd like to watch you box for real."

"Come to Coconut Casino in Bay St. Louis next Saturday night."

"I may have to pass on that. I've got a trial starting Thursday that may last over the weekend."

"You mentioned that to me. Have you learned anything about my problem?"

"I'll be honest. I haven't done anything on it yet. I'll try to make a call on Monday. But I'm really in a hole for about one more week."

"So . . . you didn't have anything special to tell me?"

"No." Tubby smiled. "I was just taking a walk and my feet led me here."

"I'm glad. I've got to work out a few more kinks before I cool off. You can watch if you like."

"Thanks, I will," Tubby said.

He sat down on a metal folding chair and watched Denise slip her mouthpiece in and climb back into the ring with a new and chunkier partner. And just then his mind took a little trip.

It was like listening to an Enya tape. Irish angels sang

sweetly and seductively in his mind, and the grunts from the ring faded away. The strong young women dancing in a slow circle jarred memories of the days that had mattered to him. Muscular brown girls, his own, splashing in the surf, getting each other's hair wet, playfully struggling over the plastic raft, calling for him to join them. And at that moment he wanted so much to step back just seven or eight years, to when the family was whole and the girls were like little fairies. He envisioned Mattie beside him, lying stomach-down on a beach towel, looking at him around the corner of her sunglasses, and for a moment the pain was too much to bear. The divorce came back, and the loneliness. Then he found his shields again, and his vision cleared. The fighters jumped back and forth in the ring, tagging each other smartly, and he sat there trying not to feel like he was the punching bag.

chapter 19

The call from Dr. Trina Tessier, associate of the late Dr. Valentine, came in around eight o'clock. After leaving the gymnasium Tubby had gone straight home and opened a bottle of bourbon. He had poured himself two on the rocks while staring at some stupid farce on the nerdwork starring adolescents who told jokes about having sex with their teachers. Easy to tune out. It was harder to go numb while waiting for the wound that had mysteriously opened in his head to heal, but he was getting there.

Funny how he would not drink much in Mike's Bar. Funny that he would be sitting home alone, drinking. Mental excursions like the one at ringside were rare now, a rabbit punch that blindsided him maybe two or three times a year, but they hurt something fierce. And now Debbie was pregnant. No two ways about it, this was his fault too. Getting a divorce had deprived her of the father figure she needed in her life. He should have stuck it out. Even if they would have committed him to a padded cell by now.

The whirring telephone interrupted his melancholy, and he pushed himself off the couch to silence it. He said hello with the phone jammed between shoulder and chin and got some more cubes from the refrigerator.

"Mr. Dubonnet?" a woman's voice inquired.

"Yes?" Tubby put away the ice tray and reached for the J. W. Dant.

"This is Trina Tessier. I met you briefly at Moskowitz lab when you came to talk to Dr. Swincter."

"Oh, yes, I remember." Tubby sat down on his kitchen stool.

"I hope I'm not calling at a bad time, but I just got off work."

"No, no, I'm just relaxing." He poured his whiskey.

"I thought I should talk to you. I know you're representing Cletus Busters. It's hard for me to believe he killed Dr. Valentine." She paused.

"I'm sure that he didn't," Tubby said.

"Do you know who did?"

"Not yet. But tell me, Dr. Tessier, why are you calling?" Tubby set his drink aside and grabbed for a pen.

"I'm just suspicious of the whole thing, really. You see, some of the research Dr. Valentine was working on was very serious. I mean, it involved the safety of a whole class of over-the-counter drugs."

"Go on."

"He had prepared a report of his preliminary findings. He showed it to me—not the findings themselves, but the report. He had printed it from his computer. It was quite thick."

"What had he found?"

"I don't know. He said he hadn't reached the end of his research, and I was too busy at the time to really talk to him."

"Do you remember anything he said?"

"Yes, that's why I remembered the conversation. He said it was the biggest discovery of his career, and it could even blow a major company off the stock exchange."

"Where is the report?"

"That's why I called. I don't know. It isn't in the lab. It's not on any part of the main computer that I can access. I thought maybe it might be locked in his office."

"At the lab? Who has the key?"

"I'm sure Dean Auchinschloss has, and maybe the police, too."

"You think this might be related to his death?"

"Hell's bells!" she shouted into the telephone, in a tone of voice she might use on an imbecile student. "It makes me pretty damn suspicious that something extremely sneaky is going on. Cletus Busters, my ass."

"Yes, indeed, Doctor, I get your point. How can we get into that office?"

Dean Auchinschloss was only too happy to let them in. He was glad that Trina Tessier had suggested it, and he was always pleased to help out in the cause of justice. He hoped they could just get to the bottom of things.

He led the way from the administrative offices of the medical school, a middle-aged curly-haired doctor in a floppy white coat, parting the sea of physicians in the corridor. Tubby had to step lively to keep up with him, and Dr. Tessier was practically trotting.

In the elevator, sharing space with a comatose patient on a gurney who appeared to have been permanently stored there, the dean talked about what a wonderful service Dr. Valentine had rendered to the hospital, how prominent had been his name, how great his contributions to the team.

"I understand that he was also on the search committee that selected you as dean," Tubby interrupted.

"That's right, so we know he wasn't perfect, ha, ha," the robust dean guffawed.

"How well did you know him, Dean?" Tubby asked as the big elevator's doors opened wide.

"Quite well, I hope." Auchinschloss ushered them into the hall and set off again. "He was one of the people who interviewed me when I came down from the Mayo Clinic. We got along immediately. He took me to lunch after I accepted the job here. We worked as colleagues for three, no, four months before his death."

"Ever know him to make any enemies?" Tubby asked, sidestepping a man with a bandage over his eyes.

"Of course not. Microorganisms and viruses were his only enemies."

And a couple thousand mice, Tubby thought. How would you like to meet that in the afterlife?

"How come his office is still here?" he asked. "After all, he's been dead for months."

They had apparently reached the right door because Dean Auchinschloss had stopped and was getting twisted up with his keys.

"First the police had it sealed. Then we had a budget review that slowed down the process of approving a replacement. I guess I really should have had it cleared out before now, but none of the other staff has been clamoring to move in."

"That's because it's an airless, windowless cubbyhole and identical to the offices the rest of us already have," Dr. Tessier explained.

She was right, Tubby saw when the dean finally got the door open. The compact space, painted white, was almost entirely filled by the institutional steel desk, the personal computer, and the printer. There was also a chair, a small bookshelf, and a dead plant.

"I think the widow took his diplomas," the dean said simply.

"Show us where you think he may have kept his report," Tubby suggested to Dr. Tessier.

Because all of them could not stand comfortably in the room together, they shuffled around awkwardly until the dean was in the hall, Tessier was seated in front of the computer, and Tubby was looking over her shoulder.

She fiddled with the keyboard until she had a menu on the screen. She worked soundlessly as Tubby watched, not understanding what he was seeing. The dean drummed his fingers on the door and hummed, the tune to "When I fall in love, it will be forever," until he noticed the pair of glares coming from within the room.

"No, not here," Dr. Tessier said finally, in exasperation.

"Let's look in the drawer," Tubby suggested.

"I didn't think of that," she said, looking embarrassed.

But no luck. There were plenty of papers stashed in there, but nothing that resembled a report on important on-going research.

"This is very strange," Tessier said. "There should be a hard copy analysis and plenty of data on the computer, too. I find it very odd that none of it is here."

"Do you know exactly what the project involved?" the dean asked.

"The only thing I know he was working on alone involved the AIDS research," Tessier said. "Your files could tell us more about that, Dean. You'd have all the grant outlines and guidelines."

"I suppose I really should go over all that," the dean said to himself. He patted his forehead to store a personal note. Tubby looked at him suspiciously, finding it hard to believe that none of this had occurred to Auchinschloss before.

As if reading his mind, the dean shrugged and put on a silly smile. The lawyer turned away.

"Was he working with you or with another doctor, like Dr. Swincter, on anything else?" Tubby asked the woman, who was still clicking away on the keyboard.

"Sure," she said. "Mrs. Smash and Mrs. Spot, two of our check-ins. Dr. Swincter was collaborating on both of those. But if there was anything unusual about those cases, Randolph would have told us so."

"That's the woman who drove into the lake and the Texas tourist who developed those odd sores in New Orleans?"

"Yes." She grinned, sending out some creases around her eyes. "How did you know?"

"I'm picking up a few things," Tubby said. "Are those two bodies still here?"

"Mrs. Spot is, I believe. The other poor woman, the one killed on the bridge, has been turned over to her family. I don't know if they buried or cremated her. I'm sure tissue samples were kept. Dr. Swincter could tell you more."

"Well, looks like this was a wild-goose chase," the dean said, looking at his watch.

"Yes, too bad, isn't it," Tubby said. "But thanks for your help, Doctor."

"It's just very strange," Tessier said, as they filed back out into the hall and Auchinschloss waved farewell. "Reports don't just disappear. I'm going to search around. And by the way, Whitney Valentine always told me he voted against bringing Auchinschloss here as dean."

"That's funny," Tubby said. "Maybe Auchinschloss never knew how Valentine voted."

"Maybe, but the dean is smarter than he looks." Tessier winked for emphasis.

"He must be," Tubby agreed.

He asked her to let him know if she found anything out, and he watched Dr. Tessier hurry down the hall. She quickly blended into the hospital landscape. He felt as out of place in his suit and tie here as he had at the gym, and he was suddenly in a rush to get outside where he wasn't afraid to catch something fatal just from breathing the air.

What had first made Tubby Dubonnet feel at home with the law were the books. Vaguely formed ideas of justice, a strong urge to make a living had caused him to enroll in law school. But it was not until his first night in the depths of the law library that he had begun to think he might actually have made a good choice. Books of legal decisions crammed the shelves, books of human stories placed before judges in hopes that they could sort out life's unfairness and find the truth.

The theory and principle behind it all occasionally escaped him, he had to admit, but he had always loved those moments in the practice of law when he had time to study those stories, stretching back to Napoleon, Justinian, and Hammurabi. They spilled out of the covers.

He was indulging himself now, taking a tour through the back pages of the Louisiana Civil Code and the annotations in the Revised Statutes in search of what dead justices might have said about a scrap involving who owned stock in a family oil business—like Denise DiMaggio's Pot O' Gold.

He thumbed through one case involving heirs to a local tobacco company. Uh-oh. This one seemed to come out the wrong way. He quickly shut that book and reached for another one.

One day, glancing through the bar journal, Tubby had seen an article that suggested that attorneys were supposed to bring contrary authority to the attention of the judge. Surely, that could not be right. What was the other lawyer supposed to be doing?

Ah, here we go. This case was much better.

"To what do I owe the honor of this call, Mr. Dubonnet?" George Guyoz sounded sarcastic, even when he was being polite.

"I'm representing Denise DiMaggio, and I understand that you're representing her uncle, Roger DiMaggio."

"Pot O' Gold Oil Company?"

"That's right."

"Isn't she the one who says she owns more stock than the company records show?"

"Correct. And she has a stock certificate for one thousand shares that your client says does not exist. But the fact is that it does exist. The company issued it to her father back in 1974, he kept it in his safe deposit box for years, and he passed it on to her in his will when he died."

"I know that's what she claims, but in the corporate books and records there is no evidence of that certificate ever being issued, and I have checked them carefully."

"Your client keeps the stock register, so I don't think that disposes of the matter by any means."

"Then we might just have to dispose of it in court."

"We might," Tubby agreed, "but there's a case you ought to know about."

"What's that?"

"*De St. Romes* versus *Levee Steam Cotton Press Company*. It's from 1879, back when the world was young. It stands for the proposition that if you possess a stock certificate for ten years, believing in good faith that you own the shares, they are yours by acquisitive prescription.''

"You mean squatter's rights for shares of stock?"

"Right on. Possess the stock certificate long enough and it's yours. And Denise and her father have possessed this one for a long, long time."

"That doesn't make a great deal of sense to me."

"Sure it does. It means that a properly issued stock certificate, signed by the right corporate officers, is good even if somebody changes the books."

"Well, I'll look at your case, but I can't believe it applies."

"It's right on point, George. It's been cited a bunch of times. Check it out, then let's settle this thing."

"Of course I'll check it out," Guyoz harumphed, "if I can pull up a case that musty on my computer. But I can't believe that it will settle anything."

I bet you're wrong, Tubby said silently after he hung up the phone. Computer?

chapter 20

Tubby enticed Detective Fox Lane to meet with him to discuss the case by offering her dinner at the Upperline. It was a very sophisticated bistro, tucked away on a back street uptown. Just the spot to lure cooperation from the most sophisticated policeman he knew. He parked in front, beneath murals of angels trumpeting up caldrons of z'herbes, and went inside.

He received a hug and an excited description of a garlic-based appetizer from the owner, shook a few hands, and got a table in the back.

He was contemplating a cocktail when Detective Lane arrived.

The waiter walked her back, and she got an interested stare from one or two of the suit-and-tie guys having an after-work restorative at the bar. At five foot ten and about 105 pounds, Fox made an impression. She was built to run. Tubby stood up to greet her.

"Hi, counselor." She beamed, showing a great talent for white teeth. "You knew just what would bring me uptown after my shift."

"I'm pretty smart, aren't I?" Tubby agreed, and held her chair to get her seated. Lane was what New Orleans called a Creole of color, meaning some European and some Af-

rican ancestry, café au lait skin, and a socially secure attitude. The message was, "We were here before you." She
was dressed nicely for having just come from work—a
smart red suit with gold buttons, only a little wrinkled from
what homicide lieutenants do all day.

"How about a drink?" he offered.

"What are you having?"

"I hadn't quite decided. I was thinking about an old-
fashioned."

"Whew. What's that?"

"Lots of bourbon and a cherry. It's something my aunts
all drink. I like to see if bartenders know how to make
them."

Their waiter returned.

"White wine for me," Lane said.

Tubby ordered his old-fashioned.

"What's the occasion, Tubby? It's been a couple of
months since I heard from you."

"Why do you think that it's anything other than me
wanting to keep up with an old law school buddy? I like
to reminisce sometimes."

"Right. You enjoyed law school about as much as I did,
Tubby. I remember how you were killing yourself all the
time, riding the Freret jet downtown between classes." She
was referring to the public transportation that ran in front
of the law school.

"And I remember how you used to come to school in
uniform, which made most of our classmates afraid to talk
to you."

"They weren't afraid. They were just happy preppy kids
and didn't know what to say to me. We didn't come from
the same part of town."

"Yeah, those were sure good times, all right."

"I got something out of it," she said.

"I'm glad to hear it. I obviously did too. My whole career. But I don't think the police department has ever ap-
preciated what they have in you."

"Why thank you, counselor. There are some who do and
some who don't. Used to be, some were suspicious of me

because I had a law degree. But you know, the only thing most people hate more than cops is lawyers, so I get the sympathy vote. I'm a double outcast. The force can relate to that.''

Tubby chuckled and sipped the drink in his hand.

"Hey, this is pretty good," he said.

"What are you going to have for dinner?" she asked.

"Oh, I thought maybe I would try the 'Filet of Gulf Fish and Salad Niçoise and Tapenade.' "

"Hmmm." She studied her menu.

"I yearn for olives," he said. "And you might like the fried green tomato with shrimp remoulade for an appetizer. It's excellent."

"What do you think of the roasted quail with grilled portobello mushrooms and bacon?" she asked.

"That's a good idea," Tubby said appreciatively. He liked his guests to eat well.

A bearded man with a black apron over his crisp white shirt took their orders. He did not hover too long.

"And?" Fox Lane prompted after the waiter left.

"Okay, I've got a case. It's in your department, but it's not one you're handling."

"And?"

"Well, I mean it's one of Detective Porknoy's files, and he is giving it his normal lack of attention and leaving his typical trail of unprofessional screwups behind him."

Detective Lane coughed and, despite herself, smiled briefly.

"Tubby," she said, "I don't want to hear your complaints about Porknoy. Other people get along with him just fine and have no problems."

"The guy's a disaster. What's your honest opinion of him?"

"No comment."

"Exactly. I think it's a wonder he's still on the force."

"He's got a lot of seniority."

"Well, anyhow, he has built a case against my client, Cletus Busters, for murdering one Dr. Valentine, and the

DA has bought it. But it's so flimsy you could almost drive a truck through it.''

"So you may win.''

"Actually, I may not. It's all circumstantial evidence, but it's the kind that a jury might convict on. The problem is, Porknoy has done nothing, so far as I can tell, to develop any other possible suspects.''

"If this is the man caught holding the frozen head, I'm familiar with the case.''

"Right, well, the victim had an adultering wife, he was in bed with one of his students, and he was involved in mysterious medical research, the reports of which are missing. Wouldn't you say there's a lot of ground that hasn't been covered here?''

"Have you brought this to Porknoy's attention?''

Tubby spread his hands. "Are you kidding? For what purpose? He has no attention span.''

"So why are you telling me?''

"I don't know. I thought maybe you could get involved. I've got the services of one investigator, I think you know Flowers, but my trial is in three days.''

"Porknoy's not going to expand his investigation at this stage of the investigation. Not right before trial.''

"Wouldn't he, if you went to him?''

The food came. "Hot plates,'' the waiter said, sliding the china onto the table.

"Looks just fine,'' Tubby said.

"My, my,'' she said.

They each tasted their dinners, and they agreed that they were pleased.

"Porknoy would be mad if I tried to tell him what to do,'' she resumed.

"But couldn't you just peek around the edges? I'd bet Porknoy's too intimidated by you to say anything. I mean, we're talking about a potential embarrassment to the whole police department. Here, let me pour you some wine.''

chapter **21**

Denise pulled the cork out of the bottle. One little glass wouldn't hurt, no matter what Coach said. She could fix a nice tomato-and-onion salad and relax for a while at least. Later on she had to go out with Carmella, her sparring partner, and she was kicking herself for agreeing to do that.

But while Denise was slicing up the tomatoes, the doorbell rang. She placed her glass on the kitchen counter and went to the front. Through the spyhole she saw the inflated face of Roger DiMaggio.

Bracing herself, she opened the door.

"By what right do you think you can have some lawyer stick his nose into my business?" her uncle demanded without preamble, barging past her into the living room. He was white-haired and red-faced, dressed in peach and green golfing attire, and built like a bear. He turned fiercely to face Denise.

"If you think you're going to scare me, you're dead wrong."

Denise kept the door open and her hand on the knob.

"I'm not trying to scare you, Uncle Roger. I just want what's fair."

"You don't know what fair is," DiMaggio yelled. "Your father didn't have the brains God gave a crawfish.

If I hadn't been around to tell him what to do he couldn't have gotten his pants unzipped, and he sure couldn't have run an oil company.''

"That's a very mean thing to say," Denise protested angrily.

"It's the damn truth!" her uncle retorted. "He never was a strong man. He couldn't even run his own house. Your mother and even pretty little you would have starved if I hadn't bought the groceries."

"We would have been better off if you had never set foot in our house."

"You don't know what you're talking about."

Denise was fighting hysteria. "Don't you think I remember what you did?"

"I never did anything that wasn't intended to help you both. Nothing that wasn't good for you."

"Then you're a liar, Uncle Roger. You made me feel guilty, and used, and worthless . . ."

Roger's face had gone from red to purple.

"Enough of that, you dumb little bitch!" he yelled. "I've got a good mind to . . ." He raised his arm as if to strike her.

Denise dropped into her stance.

"Don't even think about it," she threatened.

Slowly, Roger lowered his hand.

"You never were very smart, Denise," he said.

"But I'm getting there," she prayed through her teeth.

Roger set his jaw and stomped out the door. She immediately locked it behind him. Then she went quickly into the kitchen and downed her glass of wine.

That was about the bravest thing I ever did, she thought to herself. All these years he had been a cloud over her life. Roger's hardly secret affair with her mother. Taunting her father. Taking liberties with her. Telling them to call him Papa Dom DiMaggio.

Would she ever get free of him, and all the men like him that she kept letting in the door? Denise filled her wineglass up again.

What do you suppose Roger will do now? she asked herself.

It didn't occur to her that she might have won the round.

Watching the late news on television, his feet propped on a black leather trial case full of material about Cletus Busters, Tubby unaccountably had the feeling he was being observed. He took his eyes away from the footage of a blizzard in Buffalo and fixed them on the narrow horizontal blinds that covered the windows across the room. It was as though they were staring back at him. He shivered. Somewhere in the neighborhood a dog was barking.

Nonchalantly he stood up, left the room, and went upstairs to the table beside his bed. He pulled open the bottom drawer and carefully extracted his aging Smith & Wesson .38. He loaded it and, holding the pistol by his side, slipped back downstairs.

As quietly as he could, he turned off the lights in the kitchen and opened the back door. His yard was almost completely dark.

Cautiously Tubby stepped outside, holding the gun down. The night was cool and misty. He could feel the dew on the grass seeping into his sneakers.

Trying not to feel like a paranoid ninny, he made a furtive circuit of his home, peeking around each corner as he went, praying that none of the neighbors could see him. He checked the den window and found to his surprise that you actually could see the television show inside, if you came up close to the glass and looked through the slats at a sharp angle. If you moved your head up and down you could get a pretty good view. A car door slammed somewhere, and Tubby almost discharged his weapon into his foot.

Muttering to himself, he unlocked the front door and went back inside.

Across the street a tall figure stepped out of the shadows of a gnarled oak tree and walked swiftly down the block.

•   •   •

A light rain was falling, and Denise and her friend Carmella crossed the street in the middle of the block, dashing between the cars waiting for the light to change. Laughing, complaining, and covering their hair, they made it to the shelter of the Old Bull, a new pub boasting 101 beers. There was a crowd inside, mostly clean-cut and noisy.

Neither woman had been there before, but they tried not to show it. They moved swiftly into the place and found a couple of stools halfway down the bar.

Guys began hitting on them even before the bartender took their orders.

"Why, hey there," a charmer on the stool next to Denise, eyes a bit crossed, began.

She looked him over and raised an eyebrow.

"Can I buy you a beer?" he inquired loudly, propping himself up with his elbow on the bar.

"No, thank you," Denise said primly. "I'm waiting for someone."

She turned her back on the young man, who took it well, and said to Carmella, "I don't like it here. It's smoky."

"We don't need to stay long," Carmella said. "He should be here."

"Why did he pick this place?"

"I don't know. He just said to meet him here at eight o'clock."

"What'll it be?" the bartender asked. He was good-looking, with curly ringlets of hair trailing down his neck and a gold ring in one ear.

Carmella ordered a Pfefferneüsse Lite. Denise ordered a cranberry juice.

"I don't see how you can breathe," Denise complained again.

Carmella dug around in her purse for some bills.

"I shouldn't have asked you to come," she said, "but I was worried, that's all."

"I know," Denise said, "but you've got to get over that."

"I'm just not very good at handling things. You're a much stronger person than I am."

"That's a laugh," Denise said. She had never felt very strong. "When I was a kid they called me Little Bambino at home because that's the way I acted. I was afraid of my own shadow."

She was jostled from behind by one of a group of marauding college students, to judge from the boys' baseball caps, who were mashing their way deeper into the tavern.

"Do you have brothers and sisters?" Carmella asked.

"No. Just me. The way my father and mother got along I'm surprised they even made one baby."

"Bad, huh? My parents fought a lot too."

"Mine didn't fight. They just didn't talk to each other," Denise said. "My mother was one of those big whiners who know everything. She kept my father pretty much under her thumb."

"I guess nobody's childhood is perfect," Carmella said.

"Are you sure he said meet you here?" Denise was getting impatient.

"Yeah, when I called him and asked about the, you know, stuff, he told me about this place. He said it would be inconspicuous."

"I never did like the guy."

"I can't stand him," Carmella said.

"Can't stand who?" a voice behind them asked.

Both women jumped a little and turned around together to behold the rather pale face of Dr. Randolph Swincter.

"Can't stand who?" he repeated, moving his eyes from one to the other.

Alone at a table near the front door, Flowers grinned, then straightened out his face. He took a deep swallow from the draft beer the waitress put down before him and licked his lips in satisfaction.

Tubby got the call just as he was falling off to sleep.

Flowers told him what he had seen. The detective had followed Swincter home from work, to his apartment in the Garden District. Swincter had come out the door twenty minutes later and driven to the Old Bull Tavern on Magazine Street. Just trying to pick up girls, was Flowers's first guess, but instead of going inside immediately, Swincter had remained in his car in the parking lot. He had seemed to slouch down in his seat when two young women parked nearby, as if hiding. Intrigued, Flowers had run their plates on his mobile phone, and it turned out the car was registered to one Denise DiMaggio. Wasn't that one of Tubby's clients? Finally Swincter had gone inside and joined the two women at the bar. Yeah, they were both well-formed and muscular and could be boxers.

They had all talked for about half an hour. Swincter bought a round of drinks. And finally one of the women had gotten mad about something and stood up.

Flowers heard her tell her friend that she could go or stay, it was up to her. Reluctantly, the friend had packed up and they had both left the bar. Swincter had stayed around a little longer, not talking to anyone, and then had gone home.

"Odd coincidence," Flowers called it.

Tubby hung up, puzzled and angry. Was this Denise DiMaggio playing him for some kind of patsy?

chapter 22

"You've got a hell of a nerve!" Bennett yelled. Tubby jerked the receiver away from his ear. "Serve me with a subpoena, will you. I'm going to see that you get disbarred for this."

"There's nothing improper about subpoenaing you to testify at a murder trial, Mr. Bennett, or Dr. Bennett. I'm sorry you've taken such offense," Tubby said.

"Like hell you are. You and every other lawyer—just trying to point the finger at someone other than your own client."

"I didn't say you were guilty of anything, Doctor, but I do intend to question you about your relationship with the wife of the deceased. By the way, do you refer to chiropractors as doctors?"

"I'll have your license for this," Bennett yelled.

"Or you could explain to me now how long you've been seeing each other, and what Mrs. Valentine's husband thought about your affair."

"Why you . . ." Bennett sputtered. Then he slammed down the phone.

Tubby replaced his on the cradle gently.

"Have a nice day," he grumbled.

Cherrylynn was sitting cross-legged on the floor, sorting papers. She looked at him inquiringly.

"I could hear that from here," she said.

"He's a temperamental guy," Tubby observed mildly. "If he does that on the stand the jury might believe he killed Valentine himself."

"Do you think he did?" she asked.

"He's a pretty good prospect," Tubby said. "How are you coming?"

Cherrylynn was collating copies of more than a dozen articles and academic papers published by Whitney Valentine. Flowers had collected them with the help of a very cooperative librarian at the university. Tubby didn't know what they might reveal or even who might properly understand them.

Then the phone rang again, and the second question was answered.

"Good morning. Who is that gorgeous detective?" Dr. Tessier said cheerfully.

"So, you've met Mr. Flowers. Did he ask you any embarrassing questions?"

"Unfortunately, no. I've never met a detective before. He was far more polite than I would have expected."

"He's known for his charm. What did he ask you?"

"Oh, just about my work and who here either liked or didn't like Whitney. There's one thing I found out after he left, however, and I thought it might be important."

"What's that?"

"Dr. Valentine was scheduled to present a paper to the Neuro-Pharmacological Association meeting in Cincinnati this month. His co-presenter was Dr. Swincter. After Whitney's death, Swincter canceled out."

"I wonder why."

"I don't know. Dean Auchinschloss is the one who told me, and he didn't know either. I haven't seen Dr. Swincter to ask him. He's working today, but I'm still at home."

"I'll ask him myself. You've been very helpful, Trina. May I ask why?"

After a pause, she said, "I think it's only natural to be concerned when a colleague is murdered."

"Of course. I wish everybody felt the same way. You must have been good friends."

"Not really. We were professional competitors, in a way, but we respected each other's research skills and attention to detail. I just don't think Cletus had anything to do with it."

"Do you know him well?" Tubby found a Mardi Gras doubloon in his pocket and set it twirling around the top of his desk.

"Not at all. I mean, he did me a favor once and went to the filling station when I ran out of gas in the parking lot, and I've had a good feeling about him ever since. But that's about it."

"Maybe you could be a character witness at his trial."

"I've done it before," she said. "Cletus got caught one time letting the laboratory mice out of their cages. I put in a good word for him with the personnel department. That's probably why they didn't fire him."

"Does Cletus know that?"

"I don't think so."

"I was just wondering," Tubby said. He watched the doubloon sail off the desk and land on the carpet by Cherrylynn. "I've compiled a dozen or so articles Dr. Valentine wrote. Would you have time to look at them and tell me more or less what they mean?"

"Sure, if you have your detective bring them over to me."

"I think I can arrange that." He hung up smiling.

He told Cherrylynn that Dr. Trina Tessier seemed to be smitten by Flowers. He was a little amused by how unamused she was.

She brightened up a little when he asked her to beep Flowers on his cellular phone and see if he could nose around Cletus's neighborhood some more and recruit a couple of character witnesses.

"I'm going over to Moskowitz lab and try to track down Dr. Swincter again. Can you hold the fort here?"

"Like always," she said, in a not exactly happy tone he couldn't quite interpret.

"And please see if you can find Mickey," he requested. "We could sure use some help."

"Sorry to intrude," Tubby said to the doctor he had startled, and who was looking at him fiercely over his glasses.

"I'm rather busy, Mr. Dubonnet. This is really not a good time."

"I understand, and I wouldn't bother you if it wasn't important."

"Are you responsible for this?" Swincter asked, pulling a wrinkled yellow slip of paper from his coat pocket.

"Is that a subpoena? Yes, I'm afraid I am."

"I have two classes to teach on Thursday. I really can't be bothered with going to court for this nonsense."

"It's not nonsense. A man is on trial for his life."

"That may be, but you understand I think he's guilty. I don't see what I have to add."

"I'm not sure yet either, Doctor. But I'm trying in a very short amount of time to get an understanding of your colleague's life and work because I don't believe Cletus killed him. Someone else did."

"Any leading candidates?"

Tubby nodded his head. "A couple, maybe. I do have a question for you."

"What's that? And I also am short on time."

"You and Dr. Valentine were to present a paper at a conference in Cincinnati earlier this month."

"Yes, that's right." Swincter took off his glasses and rubbed the lenses on his white sleeve.

"And then, after his death, you canceled the appearance."

"Yes, that's right again. The research that was the subject of that presentation was incomplete when Whitney died, and I did not have the time to wrap it up on my own."

"What was the research about?"

"Nothing that would interest you. It had to do with the

metabolic effects of a certain class of drugs. It was really Whitney's baby, not mine."

"Yet he was giving you equal credit."

"Yes, we had that kind of a relationship."

"That's unusual isn't it? I thought academia was a dog-eat-dog world."

"In the liberal arts maybe, but in the sciences we are far more cooperative than that."

"Had Valentine written up a report of his experiments?"

"Not that I know of."

"Surely he must have recorded his data somewhere."

Swincter put his glasses on again and focused on the lawyer. "I would think so. He used notebooks. And, of course, his computer."

"All that seems to be missing."

"I can't explain that, Mr. Dubonnet. Naturally we'll try to reconstruct the data when time permits. But why the great interest?"

"It's just a mystery, that's all. Did he use animals in his research?"

"Quite a few, actually. He was a great rat slayer. He treated them almost as if they were, what's the word, vermin?"

"I see you're titillated by people's squeamishness where animal research is concerned."

"Don't get me started on that debate. I know I'm a monster in some people's eyes. Now please excuse me and let me get back to my work."

"Did Dr. Valentine's research have anything to do with any of your cadavers here? The tourist from Texas, the woman who drove off the bridge?"

Swincter glared at him.

"No!" he said, and turned back to his project, which involved doing something malicious to a small rodent pinned to a dissecting board.

Tubby gulped.

"I wonder, Doctor," Tubby pressed on, "do you know a young lady named Denise DiMaggio?"

Swincter looked up, lost for a moment. Then he set his narrow jaw.

"I don't think so," he said through pinched lips.

"She's a woman you might have met at a bar or something," Tubby said.

"I can't believe this. Are you having me followed?" Swincter demanded. Tubby was slightly nervous about the scalpel in the doctor's hand.

"I just wondered what you all talked about," he said.

"This is preposterous. I want you out of my laboratory!" Swincter's voice was so tight it squeaked.

"Very well," Tubby said politely, and beat it out the door with as much dignity as possible.

Was that a total waste of energy? he asked himself.

Back at the office, Tubby found Cherrylynn at her desk, staring sadly off into space. She told him that Magenta Reilly had called Dubonnet & Associates to protest the subpoena and had become very upset when she recognized Cherrylynn's voice.

"I feel terrible," his secretary moaned. "Magenta was really bent out of shape—like hysterical. I'm afraid she might do something drastic."

"I certainly hope not," Tubby said. It seemed to him that this had already been a very long day.

"I'm going to close my door and just try to think awhile," he said. "I don't want to talk to anyone on the phone unless it's very important."

He had just hung up his coat and sunk down at his desk when Cherrylynn beeped and asked whether a call from Detective Fox Lane was important. He sighed and said yes.

"Hello, Officer Lane. How are you this afternoon?" he asked.

"Ready for a vacation. I have two pieces of information for you. As you know, it is improper for me to communicate directly with defense counsel about a case under active investigation."

"I don't think it's improper, Fox. I just think it may be against your policy."

"That's a fine distinction, but anyway, here's what I have for you, confidentially. First, the other doctor who worked with the decedent, what's his name, Swincter?"

"Yeah."

"What kind of name is that?"

"Beats me."

"Anyhow, he has a large bank balance, like half a million dollars."

"Where did he get it?"

"I have no idea. Lieutenant Porknoy didn't think it worthwhile to follow up. Actually, the only way he found out about it was, he did a routine request to the university credit union about your client Cletus Busters's accounts, and they screwed up and gave him a printout of the entire department."

"How recently did the money go in?"

"No idea. All Porknoy got were balances."

"That could be anything, I guess. But thanks anyway. What did Cletus's account show, by the way?"

"About three hundred dollars."

"Figures. You said you had two things for me."

"Yeah. Number two is, Mrs. Valentine has an arrest record."

"Really? What for?"

"Assault on her husband. Almost two years ago. He was the complainant. Then the case was dismissed."

"That's very interesting. Do you have the file and the police report?"

"That would be in the warehouse somewhere."

"And Officer Porknoy didn't think that was worthy of following up either?"

"How'd you guess? Anyway, that's all I've got for you. Trial is when?"

"Jury selection starts the day after tomorrow."

"Well, if your man did it, I hope he gets the death penalty, but at least he ought to have a fair shake."

"Yeah, thanks. You're a pal."

He hung up and leaned back in his chair, eyes toward the ceiling. "Now let's think this thing through," he said out loud.

But it was not going to be that way. The intercom beeped again.

"Collect call from the jail," Cherrylynn reported. She knew he took calls from the jail.

He picked up.

"Tubby, it's me, Mickey."

"What's wrong, man?"

"I got pulled over for DWI."

"Aw, shit."

"Yeah, I know. Can you get me out of here?"

chapter 23

"Open the door, Harold," Tubby yelled while he clanged the knocker on the wood. He was at Debbie's apartment building. It was a place with lots of palm trees and a pool. He knew if he kept pounding, heads would peek out up and down the hall. "It's your old brother-in-law, Tubby."

Finally the door swung open, and Harold, unwrinkled and sandy-haired, flashed his lustrous, innocent smile and emerged into the light.

"Come on in, Mr. Tubby. It sure is good to see you. I was just about to call you for a job reference. I'm trying to get hired at that shoe store, High Top Heaven—"

"You're looking peaked, Harold," Tubby interrupted, staring past him into the gloom of Debbie's apartment.

"Don't you ever open the blinds or turn on the lights?"

"Well, I just got up. I was feeling real sick last night and couldn't sleep."

"Harold," Tubby said. "Please sit down."

They both sat. Harold was posed at the edge of the sofa, clenching his hands between his knees.

"You were supposed to stay in Hawaii, Harold. Why didn't you?"

"Well, actually, Mr. Tubby, I ran out of money. I got the check you sent me, and I had an apartment and everything. But there was a fire in the building, and it completely cleaned me out. I had a real nice job, too, making these Hula Balls, which are like Hawaiian snowballs, down on the beach, but this hellacious storm came through and blew over the snowball stand and just about everything else over there. You might have read about it.''

"No. No, I didn't. Do you have any plans, other than to stay here in Debbie's apartment?''

"Sure, I'm planning to get a job and get back on my feet just as soon as I can.''

"Why are you here, in the dark, Harold?''

"I told you. I just got up.''

"Look, is anybody after you?''

"What do you mean?''

"Like, is anybody after you? Anybody you may have ripped off? Are the police looking for you?''

"Mr. Tubby, would I be staying here with my niece, your daughter, if that was the case?''

"Yes, you probably would. Have you ever been in treatment?''

"For what?''

"For drugs. Let's not bullshit here. For marijuana or crack or whatever you're stringing yourself out on.''

"Hey.'' Harold looked insulted. "I drink a couple of beers, but I'm off the drugs now.''

"Because there are lots of programs. Hell, New Orleans is full of them. I could even help you a little bit with the cost.''

"I would definitely appreciate a loan to tide me over,'' Harold said earnestly.

"You are not getting my drift.''

"I'm off the crack, truthfully, Mr. Tubby. I've even been thinking about volunteering for one of those counseling programs where they go to the high schools and stuff and tell kids about the evils of dope, you know.''

"You can't stay here, Harold.''

"I'm not going to be around long, Mr. Tubby.''

Tubby glared at the carpet and around Debbie's apartment. It was sparsely decorated with girl things—a color

TV, a wicker chair, some flowers in a vase, a macramé wall hanging. He saw a hair dryer he thought belonged to Christine, but he did not pause to examine the implications of that. When Debbie was home, the room looked sweet and cheerful. With Harold there in the dark, it looked exposed and cheap.

"How about the Army, Harold? Have you ever thought about that? Get a skill. They pay for your education when you get out."

"Yeah, I'm definitely thinking about that if this shoe salesman deal doesn't work out."

Tubby left after that. He guessed there was nothing to be done until Debbie, or maybe Christine, decided to kick Harold out. It was her house, not Tubby's, but he could happily handle the eviction.

In the Upper Pontalba Building, two men stared at each other over a crystal vase of red camellias on the coffee table.

"I think he's getting too damn close," Mr. Flick finally said. "The risk of him running around loose is too great!"

"So what are you telling me to do?" Walter asked him.

"Take him out of the picture."

"Permanently? Or do you want me just to put him in a coma for a while?"

"Either one would be fine. Whatever you think is best, Walter. It would be in everyone's best interest if this fellow Dubonnet, or whatever his name is, were sidelined. So to speak. But it should be an accident, of course—routine street violence, perhaps."

"I can handle that."

"You'll do it personally?"

"That's what I get paid for, boss."

"Take care of this and you're due for a raise."

Walter took one of the camellias from the vase and smelled it.

"Odorless," he said. The crooked twist his pretty lips took might have scared a child.

"Not to me it's not," Flick said.

• • •

Cherrylynn parked her slightly ratty Datsun across from Magenta Reilly's apartment on Jeff Davis Parkway. Distressed as she was, she didn't even get mad at herself for dragging her car's tender sidewall along the ragged granite curb.

She hurried across the street. The lights of a passing car caught her, and some teenagers yelled something she didn't want to hear. She rang the bell but no one answered, so she rapped on the door.

Footsteps came down the hall, and a voice asked, "Who's there?"

"It's Cherrylynn," she replied. "We met at the laundromat."

"Go away. I don't want to talk to you," Magenta said.

"Please let me apologize. I feel terrible."

"Go away right now."

"Please. I know you're mad at me, but I do want to say I'm sorry. Could you at least let me do that?"

The door opened a crack. A slice of Magenta's face appeared, and she had been crying. Cherrylynn offered a big, miserable smile.

"I really do apologize," she said. "Could I come in for just a minute? I'm not a bad person."

"I suppose," Magenta said.

Cherrylynn stepped quickly inside.

"I shouldn't have fooled you last weekend. I know it was the wrong thing to do."

"Who are you really?" Magenta demanded.

"I'm a legal secretary for Mr. Tubby Dubonnet. He's the lawyer for Cletus Busters."

"The man who killed Whitney?"

"Mr. Dubonnet doesn't believe he did it, Magenta. We're trying to find out who really did. And I guess I was just playing at being detective when I talked to you. I'm not very good at it."

"I'm sure you found out everything you wanted to know about me." Magenta pouted.

"Yes, I did. I found out that you are a very nice person, and not the sort who would kill anybody. You didn't really tell me anything confidential."

"What exactly were you trying to learn?"

"Look, may I sit down?"

"Okay, I guess."

"Thanks." Cherrylynn plopped down on the sofa.

"See, there's a real detective working for Mr. Dubonnet. His name is Flowers. Anyway, Flowers found out somehow—don't ask me how—that you and Dr. Valentine were having a relationship."

Magenta gasped.

"That's not true," she squeaked.

"It probably doesn't really matter anyway," Cherrylynn continued. "We were just trying to find out who else besides Mr. Busters would have a motive to kill Dr. Valentine, and so Mr. Dubonnet, and Flowers and me, were talking to everyone we could think of."

"I could never have killed Professor Valentine."

"Oh, I can tell that. Mr. Dubonnet also investigated Mrs. Valentine. And you know what? She was having an affair too—with a chiropractor."

"That woman is such a witch," Magenta said bitterly.

"Why do you say that?" Cherrylynn asked.

"She made his life a living hell," Magenta said.

Cherrylynn leaned forward and nodded her head.

"You don't have any coffee?" she asked.

At that moment Denise unlocked her apartment door. The lights were on inside, and the TV was blaring.

"Baxter?" she called.

"It's me," he said, getting up from his chair in front of the television.

He spread his arms, came to her, and kissed her hard. He had poured a beer or two.

He pulled her head back.

"You're late," he said.

"I'm sorry, Baxter, but let go of my hair," she began.

He slapped her across the mouth.

"Papa's home. You should be on time."

"Stop that," she cried.

"That's no way to talk to Coach," he said and pressed her roughly against the couch.

"I love you, Baxter." It was a complaint, or a question.

He grabbed her jaw in his hand so that her lips were squeezed together and her ears hurt. "So, you should do what I tell you to do," he said fiercely.

But why should I? she screamed inside.

"Ow!" she protested.

chapter 24

Y ou don't have any coffee, do you?" Flowers asked Tubby.

"I just put a pot on," Cherrylynn said. "It'll be done in a minute."

The morning was gray, and it seemed even grayer from the forty-third floor, where you could see the river, the lake, and the sky all competing for dreariness.

Tubby was still groggy from dealing with Central Lockup, springing O'Rourke from the drunk tank, which had taken until the wee hours, and Flowers looked discouraged. Only Cherrylynn seemed wide awake and full of pep.

"Now, where were we, Mr. Flowers?" Tubby asked.

"I spent too much time in Cletus's neighborhood yesterday. I found absolutely nobody who would really claim to know the man—certainly no one who would testify as to his good works and moral rectitude. One lady said he was good about picking up his trash cans after the garbagemen came. I didn't think you could use that. I also failed to find someone who could verify his whereabouts on the Friday of the murder."

"We know he went to work," Tubby said.

"Yeah, but I thought maybe we could show what he did

before and after his shift—like maybe he didn't act like a man who had just murdered someone and stuffed him in a freezer. But no one could, or would, tell me anything."

"It's a real problem," Tubby said, "that Cletus has no recollection at all about what he did on the Friday of the murder. He just says he went to his job, but he can't remember any details, or even what else he did that day. I suppose it's not so strange. It all happened four months ago."

"People are always skeptical when the accused has no alibi," Flowers commented.

"Hell, I'm skeptical, and I'm his lawyer. But I guess it's not surprising. How many of us recall what we did last week?"

Cherrylynn and Flowers swapped glances.

"I usually do, Mr. Dubonnet," she said.

Flowers just shrugged.

"Well anyway, where do we go from here? Who's got an idea?"

"I don't have any ideas, boss," Cherrylynn said, "but Magenta Reilly told me that Dr. Valentine's wife has been going out with Bennett for months. She didn't keep it a secret from him, but she sure did from everyone else because she wanted alimony if he sued her for a divorce. She told him she didn't care if he left, so long as he paid her a lot every month for support. She claimed she put him through medical school and he owed her. She was real abusive, and even would attack him physically, I mean."

Tubby couldn't get over his surprise. "You got all this from the medical student you had coffee with?" he asked.

"Yes sir," she said proudly. "And Dr. Valentine also told Magenta he was going to leave his wife, just as soon as he finished some very important project. He said he had to concentrate on his work to get it done, but after that the marriage was all over. He was going out the door."

"Valentine confided all this to Magenta?"

"Yes sir. Valentine even told Magenta he loved her. She's pretty broken up."

Tubby kept staring at his secretary, but his mind was elsewhere.

Cherrylynn and Flowers looked at each other, and around the office, and at their hands.

"Do we know where Bennett and Mrs. Valentine were on Friday when Valentine was killed?" he finally asked.

"Bennett says he worked at his clinic until five-thirty, then went home and watched TV. Ruby Valentine says she finished her shift at the hospital at seven o'clock, then she also went home and watched TV. The police verified that both of them were at their jobs, like they said. Since the coroner couldn't be very specific about the time of death, due to the frozen nature of the body, I couldn't think of any more probing questions to ask."

"In your opinion, could either of them have gotten into Moskowitz lab without being seen?"

"Going by my own experience, Tubby, you can get into that joint just about anytime without being noticed. You may be seen, but if you dress like a doctor or a nurse, and don't ask directions, nobody is likely to remember you."

"I agree," Tubby said. "I don't think they even remembered me." He sounded offended. "So," he concluded, "we have nowhere to go."

"There's the missing medical research Valentine was working on," Flowers suggested.

"Right," Tubby said. "Dr. Tessier has offered to bone up on Valentine's past writings. Maybe that will point us somewhere. She especially asked that you drop off the copies personally."

"They all axed for me," Flowers sang.

"Go to it then," Tubby said, "and let's try to get back together early afternoon. I'm going to see Cletus now."

"How's Mr. O'Rourke?" Cherrylynn asked.

"My co-counsel is probably waking up now with a monster hangover. It took me till after three o'clock this morning to get him out of jail, and he looked pretty bad. I took him home. He said he would come here this afternoon, but who knows."

"What should I do with him if he shows up?" Cherry-lynn asked.

"Just put him in the conference room and ask him to read the file. Maybe he can figure something out."

Nobody would venture an opinion on that.

"He used to be a good lawyer," Tubby said. "Really."

"You want me to talk to Denise DiMaggio about how she knows Dr. Swincter?" Flowers asked quietly.

Tubby sighed. "No," he said. "I guess I'll try to see her after I pass the jail."

"It ain't gonna be long now," Cletus said, "until they find me guilty and fry me."

"It's lethal injection now, Cletus—and you're a long way from that. You are smart to face the possibility though. You have an option to consider too. You could plead guilty. I believe we could make a deal for life without parole—maybe even forty years straight time."

"Screw that. I ain't killed nobody."

"That's fair, Cletus. I always think it's bad policy to plead guilty when you're innocent. This is a tough one to handicap, though. Being conservative, I'd say that the odds are sixty to forty in favor of you getting convicted. And if you're convicted, I'd say the odds are fifty-fifty in favor of you getting the death penalty."

"What kind of lawyer I got? A hopeless one?"

"No. Just straight up with you." Tubby tried to hold Cletus's eyes with his own. "You haven't got an alibi. You had a motive because Valentine wanted to get you fired. You were there the night of the crime. You got caught with the man's head in your hands. The district attorney will make a very entertaining speech about that."

"And what you gonna be doin'? Scratchin' your head? Watchin' the bees?"

Tubby slapped his palm on the cracked Formica. "Are we having some kind of personality conflict? Or are you like this with everybody?"

"Okay, man, say your piece."

Tubby took a deep breath.

"Is there somebody, like your mother, or a brother or sister, who could speak well of you in the courtroom?"

"My mother died last year, and I don't know where my brothers and sisters live. I stay to myself."

"How about your patients, the ones you do healings for?"

"They come to me for cures. I don't go to them. They respect what I can do, but I wouldn't have them coming down here to say anything about that in court."

"It would help if somebody would speak for you."

"They ain't nobody who will."

"Dr. Trina Tessier says she will—all because you helped her when she ran out of gas."

"She's all right," Cletus conceded. "I like her okay. She can testify if she wants to."

"Thanks. Have you had any luck summoning up the spirits? Have you had any visions about who might have done this crime?"

"You can make fun of me, but I got my ideas about it," Cletus said.

"Tell me."

"I'll tell 'em when I get on the witness stand tomorrow."

"I don't think you'll be taking the witness stand, Cletus. If you do, they can ask you all about your prior bust for drugs, not to mention your religious practices. They'll make it sound like Valentine was part of a ritual sacrifice."

"I will tell my side of it," Cletus said hotly.

"Give me a hint. What would you say?"

"I'd talk about the laws of the universe. The order and the balance, and what happens when you violate that order, like when you gives lots of animals diseases and kill them."

"Yeah? What happens?"

"You get punished. That's what I'm gonna say."

Not if I can help it, Tubby thought.

"So you think Valentine was punished for killing mice? Who did the punishing?"

"It don't matter who done it, just that it got done."

"You don't care that they're blaming you for it?"

"Sure, I care, but that's just their system, man. I'm the handiest one to blame."

As Tubby walked out through the sliding bars he was thinking that Cletus at least had that part right.

Denise told Tubby she could meet him after she finished teaching at three o'clock. She suggested the Daily Grind coffee house on Magazine Street. He said okay because it was close to where he lived. He was astonished upon arrival to find chicory coffee on the menu, unheard of in a "gourmet" coffeehouse, and he was enjoying the strong brew when she walked in. She waved at him on her way to the counter.

"Howya doing?" he said when she brought her mug and saucer to the table. "What's that you got?"

"It's a blueberry scone," she said. "Want to try it?"

She passed her plate to him, and he pinched off a warm crumb from the biscuit.

"It's not real sweet," he mentioned.

"No, not very," she said.

So what's the point? he wondered, but Denise seemed to think it was just right.

"You never had a scone before?" she asked.

"Not that I recall," he said. He did not expect they would ever form a regular part of his diet.

"You said you wanted to talk to me," Denise reminded him.

"Yeah. You told me that you came to me because Monique Alvarez recommended me."

"That's right," Denise said.

"It had nothing to do with any of the cases I'm working on?"

"No," she said, putting a square white napkin carefully under her cup.

"Well then, what the heck were you doing meeting Randolph Swincter at a bar the other night?"

He said it quietly enough, and she did not collapse in shock, but something about his tone or her gasp penetrated the mellow atmosphere of the establishment, and caffeine fanciers at two nearby tables paused in their conversations to see how she would answer.

"I, uh, went there with a friend of mine," Denise said, laying her spoon neatly on the napkin. She raised her eyes to Tubby's as the strains of violins on the sound system got loud enough to drown out whispers. "I didn't know when I first came to see you that the murder case you told me about was Dr. Valentine's."

"But now you do."

"I know, but me going to that bar had nothing to do with your case."

"Tell me about it anyway," he insisted.

"I used to see Whitney Valentine at bars," she said. "He used to give, like, these health lectures, on aerobics and stuff, and he talked to us at the gym one time. He was real good-looking and not shy, if you know what I mean."

Tubby frowned. "No, what do you mean?"

"He asked all the girls out. Me, Carmella, the others too. I mean, he seemed to have lots of money, and he liked to party."

"Did you party with him?"

"I went out with him on maybe one date. Honestly, Mr. Dubonnet. But Carmella started going out with him."

"And so, what?" Tubby asked.

Denise lowered her voice so that he had to lean forward to hear her.

"He gave her drugs, like prescription painkillers. And he gave her stuff that doesn't show up on the drug scans they make us take."

"Do you all use drugs?" Tubby asked in dismay.

"No," Denise said, raising her right hand. "I don't. Carmella is the main one I know who does."

"Couldn't you be kicked out of boxing for hanging around drugs, or protecting people who do?"

"Yeah. I don't know. Maybe."

"Well, why did you meet Swincter?"

"Carmella asked me to. After Valentine got killed, she couldn't get her stuff anymore. It was okay for a while because she had a bunch stored up. But when she ran out she called up Valentine's partner to see if she could get some more from him."

"How did she know Swincter?"

"He was always hanging out with Whitney. We all knew him. He was just, like, this guy that Dr. Valentine had with him when we went out at night."

Tubby rested his chin on his fist.

"How did Swincter react to this request for drugs?"

"Okay. He told Carmella to meet him at the bar. She was afraid to go by herself because Swincter is a little bit creepy, and she got me to go with her. That's all there was to it."

"What happened at the bar?"

"Nothing. All he wanted to do was hit on us. He wasn't going to give Carmella anything. I think he was suspicious about something. He made what I considered to be a crude pass. I got mad and left."

"That's it?" Tubby asked.

"Really," she said.

He looked out the window at an attractive young woman herding two girls in pink ballerina outfits past the police station across the street. Mothers were getting younger and younger, he reflected.

"I can't stand it when clients lie to me," he said.

"I'm not lying," she protested.

"It's not that I have so many clients I can turn away all the ones I don't personally like. It's not necessary that I like them all. But they've got to tell me the truth. Generally speaking, I don't care if you're guilty as hell if you tell me. I'm not wasting my time and my reputation on people who lie to me."

"I promise you." Denise looked like she might cry. "I'm not."

Two young women studying Civil Procedure at the next table glowered at Tubby. He glowered back.

"Okay, okay," he said. "I believe you. I'm just too

trusting sometimes, and I don't want to be taken advantage of.''

"I'm the same way,'' she sniffled. She rubbed her nose with her hand. She had some muscles in those arms. "I just want to be liked. I seem to meet all the wrong people . . . Why is it so hard?''

"Eat your scone,'' he said. "Tell me what you taught your students today.''

Denise sat back in her chair and took a deep breath. Then she laughed. "I showed them some mathematical puzzles where you can prove that two and two doesn't always add up to four.''

After he said goodbye to Denise, Tubby drove slowly down Magazine Street. He had told Denise he believed her, but it would have been more truthful to say he wanted to believe her. He saw the Open sign on the window of Tee Eva's Famous Pie Shop and skidded to the curb.

He tapped on the sliding glass window, trying to look past the newspaper clippings and photos of famous people who liked her pralines and jambalaya to see if anyone was in the dim kitchen.

The glass slid back, and Tee Eva, gold lamé sun hat with a visor on her head and gold-framed eyeglasses on her nose, smiled at him.

"Hi, darlin','' she said. "You must be hungry.''

"Have you got your pecan and sweet potato pies today?'' he asked.

"Sure,'' she said. "I got sweet potato, pecan, or pecan-and-sweet-potato. Which would you like?''

"I'll take one of each,'' he said, and watched the slender woman move around her small kitchen collecting his pies and a plastic Time Saver bag to put them in.

"Have you ever had a scone?'' he called through the window.

"You mean those English tea cakes? Sure I've had them.''

"Really? Where have I been?'' Tubby said.

"They ain't exactly New Orleans, honey," she consoled him.

"Do you like them?" Tubby asked, taking his bag.

"To me, scones is not a big deal," she said, and favored him with a sparkling smile.

"Okay," Tubby said.

Tubby reached Monique on the phone.

"It's been too long," he said. "How's the bar? How's Lisa?"

"We're doing just fine, Mr. Tubby. I want you to come and visit us."

"I plan to do that soon, just as quick as things settle down here a bit."

"I want to thank you for helping out my friend Denise."

"Let me ask you a question about her. Is she all right? I mean, do you trust her?"

"Denise? Sure. I mean I haven't known her very long, but. . . . Why do you ask that?"

"It's just that she dated the deceased in a murder case I'm taking to trial. It's a bad coincidence."

"Well, I wouldn't know anything about that. I met her when I started going to the gym to work out. She's been completely straight with me. She's from Vacherie, and I'm from Alabama, but we had a lot of the same stuff in the past. I think she lacks confidence, is all."

"What's that got to do with anything?"

"For some women, it has a lot to do with everything," Monique said angrily.

"Sorry," Tubby retreated. "I mean, what's it got to do with being honest?"

"I don't know, but she had a really screwed-up childhood. I don't think she had anything like a model home life. And being from the boondocks, she thinks she's dumb. She doesn't even realize she's pretty. She needs lots of encouragement."

Jeez. He was getting her whole life story.

"So the connection is, you like her," Tubby said.

"Yes, I do," Monique replied.

"So now I feel better," Tubby said.

"She's got a bad situation going right now, too."

"Oh? What's that?"

"She's been dating her trainer, this guy Baxter Sharpe."

"Uh-huh."

"I think he beats her up."

"I see."

"Yeah. I don't know what you can do about it."

"I'm not sure either. Why does she put up with it?"

"I can't answer that. I don't think she really loves him. Maybe it's a disease some women contract."

"You know something about that."

"Yeah, and I got well."

"I don't know if I can help with that." Tubby shrugged, even though he was on the phone.

"I just wanted you to know."

"Okay."

"Don't forget where I am."

"Never."

They hung up. Don't ever say there's no women's mafia, he thought.

chapter **25**

Coming through the door of Dubonnet & Associates, O'Rourke looked a lot better than he had at Central Lockup. His hair was combed, his coat was on straight, and the storm clouds had cleared out of his eyes. Tubby asked everyone to join him in the conference room. Flowers overfilled his chair and put his back to the window. Cherrylynn sat across the table from him. Mickey shuffled through the file.

"Jury selection should take all of tomorrow," Tubby began. "It will just be bad luck if the trial gets under way before Judge Stifflemire wants to adjourn for the afternoon. And before our side starts, the judge will hear my motion to suppress Cletus's prior drug conviction. So we hope it's Friday before the state begins to put on its case. That will take a day. So maybe we get the weekend to keep digging."

No one said anything. O'Rourke kept turning pages.

"I'll plan to cross-examine Detective Porknoy, unless you want to, Mickey."

Mickey kept his eyes down and shook his head.

"Okay, but you can have the medical examiner or, if you want, the security guard."

Mickey shook his head again. "I don't want to cross-examine anybody," he said morosely.

"Man, you can do this," Tubby said, to encourage him. "It's your case. You're lead counsel."

Mickey laughed. It was not a pleasant sound.

"God help Busters," he said, "if this was really my case. I don't want to take any witnesses, gang. I would just embarrass myself."

"There's too much here for one lawyer to handle, Mickey. I need help too."

Mickey looked hopeless.

"Look," Tubby said. "Here's the deal. You prepare, just like you were going to cross-examine the security guard, and you also prepare a direct examination of Ruby Valentine. Just so you'll be ready if I need you."

"All right, I suppose." Mickey stood up. "But you better not count on me. I know I'm a damn wreck. I can accept that. But I don't believe I could accept it if Cletus Busters got the death penalty because of my screwups."

"So, you'll do your best to get ready?" Tubby pressed.

"Yeah," Mickey said, and he straightened his tie and left.

"He'll blow the entire case," Flowers declared flatly.

"Maybe not," Tubby insisted. "If he gets motivated he might do okay."

"My money's still on you," Flowers replied. "By the way, you want me to pry any further into Denise DiMaggio's nocturnal affairs?"

Tubby stared over Flowers's shoulder and shook his head. "No. I'm going to take a chance on this one and just let it go."

Flowers acknowledged that statement by clearing his throat.

Cherrylynn looked from one to the other, trying to figure out what she was missing. Then the telephone lit up and she went to the corner to answer it.

"It's somebody who calls himself W. D. He won't give his last name. He says you'll speak to him," she told Tubby.

"Can't be," he said. "Is this really Wild Dan?" he inquired into the telephone.

"Tubby, how's the state champion wrestler and lubricator of the wheels of capitalism doing today?"

"Oh, I'm doing great, man. Where y'at?"

"Up near Marksville. Can't say exactly where. We've got us a labor dispute among some catfish-plant workers going on."

"Are you still organizing for the union?"

"Sure, man. Still a Wobbly. And guess what, I'm coming your way."

"Oh, neat," Tubby said. The muscles in his stomach and neck tightened involuntarily. Dan's infrequent sorties into New Orleans disrupted all of Tubby's routines and threatened everything he held dear.

"Yeah, man. Got a call from some hotel bellhops. Can't say at what hotel. They want me to negotiate for them."

"When are you planning to get here?"

"Should be in a couple of weeks. Right now we got these fish slime bosses by the catfish nuggets. We ought to be able to wrap it up real soon. Then I'll just slide on down to the Big Easy. Look for me on your doorstep."

"Well . . ." Tubby said.

"Gotta go. Don't want to stay too long in one place. See you when I do."

"See you."

"Who was that?" Cherrylynn politely asked, when she tired of watching him staring at the handset.

"Just an old friend of mine from college coming to town. You might have to run things here for a couple of days."

She shot him a look over her shoulder as if to say, What else is new?

"He's a real story in himself," Tubby chuckled. "Well, we can forget about him for now."

There really wasn't much else to talk about. Tubby told them he was going to take a drive—just to clear his head before going home to rest. He told Flowers and Cherrylynn to lock up and do something relaxing for the evening.

•   •   •

"Is there anything else I can do for you?" Cherrylynn asked Flowers after her boss left.

The detective stretched and yawned.

"No, not that I can think of," he said. "I think I may be off for the night."

"Me too," Cherrylynn said.

"Sometimes it's like this. Hurry, hurry, then . . . nothing." He spread his hands. "All you can do is wait to see what happens in court."

"Mr. Dubonnet seems discouraged. He's not usually like that."

"Oh, Tubby is an odd bird," Flowers said. "He has a way of pulling things out of his hat."

Cherrylynn smiled. "You're right. But when he gets down in the dumps, that's when I start to worry."

"Hey, that's your job," Flowers said. He stretched again and stood up.

"I suppose I'll head out," he said.

"Me too," she said. "Maybe get something to eat." She took a breath. "You want to join me? We could have a drink somewhere?" She blushed.

"I'll have to pass tonight, Cherrylynn," Flowers said. "I have other duties."

"Sure, okay," Cherrylynn said. "Well, good night then."

"See you in court," he said, and soared out of the door with his long gliding stride.

She stared at the space he had left, then started tidying the place up for tomorrow.

Outside the St. Charles Avenue entrance to the Place Palais building where Dubonnet & Associates had its home was a watering hole called the Sandy Bar. It was for securities brokers and young professionals who wanted an altitude adjustment before rolling on home in their fancy cars. Along with a string of losers, Cherrylynn had met a couple of nice people there, and she knew the bartenders. One of them, a young Irish rover with an earring, smiled at her when she walked in and beckoned her toward a tall chair. She looked around to check out the crowd and saw

Flowers and Trina Tessier laughing together at a corner table, over the warm glow of a candle flickering in a red goblet. Cherrylynn made an abrupt U-turn and departed, feelings bleeding and brokenhearted again.

And I'm such a pretty girl, too, she thought.

chapter 26

Tubby's drive took him to Mike's Bar, where he indulged his own weakness at a table in the corner by himself. Larry filled him a glass whenever he raised a finger, and Tubby raised all the fingers on one hand.

He thought about how Cletus Busters's miserable life was in his hands and how he was sitting here like an asshole getting plastered. A fear he hadn't encountered since his law school exams had him in its grip. The trouble was, he had no defense for Cletus. He might lose the case. He could not remember ever approaching trial so empty-handed. And Tubby had no defense for himself. He raised another finger, and Larry shuffled his way.

Finally, feeling ill, he waved ta-ta to his bartender and stepped clumsily into the night.

"Steady as you go," he instructed himself as he stumbled on a piece of concrete jutting out of the broken sidewalk. The street was quiet. A cat hissed at him and leapt off the hood of his Spyder.

It was blocking a fire hydrant, but the meter maids did not venture into this neighborhood.

"I'm all right," he said out loud as he slid behind the wheel.

He believed Tchoupitoulas Street might be the safest way

home for him, meaning the road less traveled by policemen and other motorists. It ran beside the railroad tracks and the wharves, following the river's curve, and though it had major potholes, he knew where most of them were.

After a few misfires, the Spyder's turbo-charged six got going. He found WWOZ on the radio, an old blues show hosted by John Sinclair. Tubby himself had the blues so bad he wanted to point his car toward Texas and cruise until he ran out of gas.

With that destination in mind, he laid a black streak of rubber and shot off into the darkness. He skipped a stop sign and rounded the corner onto Tchoupitoulas Street in a graceful slide.

Headlights came up fast in his rearview mirror.

Cops, Tubby thought, but relaxed as the other car pulled beside him to pass on the narrow rocky street.

"Goddamn maniac," he griped.

It was passing too close. Tubby almost lost control of the wheel as the big car broadsided his, inches from his shoulder. His little sports car hopped the curb onto the broken, grassy sidewalk.

Trash cans and telephone poles loomed ahead, and he zipped past them, nicking the wooden steps of a shotgun house built close to the street. Tubby's mouth was open, and maybe he was yelling. He fought his way back into the roadway and jammed hard on his brakes. The big car behind him clipped one of the Spyder's taillights and sent the unstable sports car skidding cockeyed down the lonely street.

Tubby straightened out, downshifted, and shot a quick glance behind him. He couldn't see who the other driver was. He shifted up, and the Spyder roared down the street, fender flapping, with the other vehicle in pursuit.

The contest was short. The big car got on his bumper again, and when Tubby maneuvered around an asphalt crater he found himself in the wrong lane, in a neck-and-neck race again.

He got smacked soundly on the passenger side and pushed toward the truck-loading docks. He was bouncing in the seat and frantically trying to turn the wheel when his car hit the train tracks and left the ground. The Corvair sailed nicely, but landed hard with a crunch. It slid noisily over gravel, concrete, and trash and sheared along the side of a brick warehouse, trailing sparks, until it slammed into a Dumpster.

The big car that had rammed him shot past and disappeared into the night.

Tubby found that he was alive and gradually released his grip on the steering wheel. Tests showed that his toes and fingers worked. He dared gasp for air.

His car was breathing steam, but quiet had returned to the dark street.

Tubby climbed out of the wreck of his Corvair. "I guess this heap is finally finished," he told himself sadly.

He scanned the forbidding facades of the deserted warehouses and the empty street. No help was in sight.

It occurred to him that when the police came, they might take one whiff and arrest him.

Despondent over the mess his car had become, he cleaned out his glove box, stuffed the registration in his pocket, and set off limping down the street.

He knew where he could catch a bus. He only had to traverse about ten blocks of some other guys' turf.

chapter 27

In the morning, Tubby called a client of his, Adrian Du-
plessis, and told him where to find the Spyder. Adrian,
whose street name was Monster Mudbug, drove a tow truck
by trade. He was curious about what had happened, but
Tubby massaged the pain in his head and said he would
tell him later.

He drove his respectable Lincoln to work—cautiously.
He had no idea who he had tangled with the night before,
and he doubted he would ever find out. There were some
crazy people riding the streets of New Orleans.

He couldn't waste time wondering about that with his
trial starting in an hour.

George Guyoz's phone call caught Tubby just as he was
walking into his office.

Guyoz said he had read Tubby's Supreme Court case and
had to admit that it might have some passing similarity to
the facts of the Pot O' Gold stock controversy.

"In fact, they are almost exactly the same," Tubby said,
to rub it in.

"Well, there are some differences," Guyoz sniffed, "but
without wasting a lot of your time and mine arguing about
it, I think you have a fairly good position."

"Then we agree."

"I believe we might. I've explained things to my client, and he is ready to do the right thing. He will recognize his niece's one thousand shares, and she will recognize his. They will then be equal partners."

"Wait a second," Tubby said. "She also has another stock certificate for one hundred shares, so she's actually the majority stockholder."

"No, no," Guyoz protested. "He is not going to agree to that. Roger DiMaggio built the company. If your young lady wants to run it fifty-fifty, and agrees to keep her uncle on as a salaried officer, then we can make a deal. But if you expect more than that, we'll litigate till hell freezes over."

"And you'll lose."

"Maybe. Maybe not. That's a mighty old case you're relying on. I can promise you, however, that Roger Di-Maggio is not just going to bend over for his niece's benefit."

"Okay, I don't know what her reaction will be, but I understand your proposition. I'll discuss it with Denise and get back to you."

"Right. Do it quickly because there's a big oil-drilling contract under negotiation, and it cannot get finalized until we settle who owns what."

Tubby said he would respond as quickly as he could. The words "big oil-drilling contract" had an extremely nice ring to them.

Hazel Whitepod, Judge Stifflemire's secretary, unlocked the doors of Section O at nine o'clock on Thursday morning when the high-ceilinged corridors of the Criminal District Court for the Parish of Orleans were just beginning to echo with the quick footsteps of busy lawyers, the shrieks of little children, and the shuffle of orange-suited prisoners being escorted here and there in chain gangs. Jury selection for State of Louisiana versus Cletus Busters began an hour and a half later, at half past ten.

In the meantime, Tubby and Cherrylynn came chugging

up the stairs, each carrying a black leather trial case full of
Tubby's notes, a sheaf of exhibits, and a green book that
contained the Code of Evidence. There were reporters in
the hall. The TV news had stayed outside where the light
was better. "We expect to see justice done," Tubby had
grimly told them all. He was too worried about his lack of
a case to bluster any more than that.

Judge Stifflemire arrived in his chambers and Hazel
brought him some coffee in a mug that said "Krewe of
Olympians" on it. He read the society page of the newspaper, then took his coffee into his private washroom and
poured it down the sink, just as he did every morning. He
pulled his black robe over his head and checked his thinning hair in the mirror before signaling Hazel to signal the
bailiff that the judge was on his way.

"Oyez, oyez. All rise! The Criminal District Court for
the Parish of Orleans is now in session. The Honorable
Hector Stifflemire presiding. Order and silence are commanded."

"Good morning," the judge said, taking his accustomed
perch behind his mahogany bench, from which he could
see a younger version of himself, rendered in oils, hanging
on the wall in the company of judges past.

"Good morning," all the lawyers murmured, and everyone else sat down and hid.

He disposed of four guilty pleas and as many continu-
ances of motions and trials before settling down to the main
business at hand.

Cletus was in his workman's clothes, handcuffed in the
pews to the judge's right where prisoners got to wait, but
when his case was called the cuffs came off and he was
led to the counsel table where he could sit beside Tubby.
Cletus's checkered green shirt smelled like mothballs.

"Damn, they keep it cold in here," Cletus said by way
of greeting.

"You okay?" Tubby asked. It didn't seem cold to him
at all.

"Good as I'm gonna get," Cletus whispered.

Tubby nodded to Clayton Snedley, the assistant district

attorney, and the serious young woman who was his lieutenant, when they took their places at the adjoining table.

The judge cleared his throat and received everyone's attention. He scanned the room over the top of his glasses.
"Are we ready?" he asked in a booming voice.

"Yes, Your Honor," the district attorney said.

"I have a motion to suppress yet to be heard, Judge,"
Tubby said, rising to his feet.

"Yes. Well, we'll take that up after we impanel the
jury."

Stifflemire waited a moment until Tubby got seated
again.

"Let's bring 'em in," the judge shouted.

The clerk gestured to the bailiff, who gestured to the
policeman at the rear, and he pushed open the tall wooden
doors to admit the first of the herd.

"This should take all day—maybe tomorrow, too,"
Tubby confided to his client.

It took an hour and ten minutes.

The first group of twenty potential jurors yielded nine
winners. The next group filled out the dozen.

With jarring regularity, almost all of the candidates
seemed to be unemployed, retired, or otherwise available
and anxious to do their civic duty for ten dollars a day and
lunch from Mandina's. Few had the wit to come up with
an excuse that would prevent them from serving on a jury.
The only good line came from a local writer who, rubbing
his wrinkled forehead to squeeze out the words, said that
he could not differentiate between fantasy and the real
world, and that when confronted with unpleasantness, he
chose fantasy. Judge Stifflemire scolded him, and then let
him go.

The judge asked the next guy in line if he had any problem that might prevent jury service.

"Yeah, what he said," the man exclaimed hopefully,
pointing at the departing writer.

Stifflemire tossed his gavel in the air, caught it, and gave
the whole courtroom a lecture for that.

Tubby only exercised two peremptory challenges—one

on a severe French lady who glared at Cletus until she made him squirm, the other on a Presbyterian minister who benignly promised to look upon all witnesses with equal love and trust. Tubby was afraid the pastor might disapprove of Cletus's personal religious preferences if by some unhappy turn of events these came out in court.

The district attorney excused a black man who seemed to do nothing more offensive than answer the judge's questions in an angry tone. Tubby let it pass. That's what peremptory challenges were for.

The rest the judge released because they had recently had a loved one murdered, because they would lose their jobs if they missed work, or because they seemed to have difficulty comprehending questions in the English language.

Tubby was satisfied when it was done. He had ten blacks and two whites. You always made those kinds of observations in New Orleans, even if you didn't know how to interpret the data. It was a mixed group—a taxi driver, a housewife or two, an unemployed barber, a night clerk at a French Quarter hotel, an old seaman, a retired nurse. Cherrylynn was taking copious notes about everyone for him to study later.

Time for lunch? Nope.

"Let the jurors go out and relax," Stifflemire said. "Let's have your motion, Mr. Dubonnet."

"Ah yes, Your Honor," he began after the jury shambled out. "The state has noticed its intent to present evidence of the defendant's prior conviction for sale of a controlled substance. It's entirely unrelated to the matter at hand and could obviously be very prejudicial to the jury. You have my brief, Judge. We move to suppress the prior."

"I follow, Mr. Dubonnet. How do you respond, Mr. Snedley?"

"We're going to show that the motive for the defendant's murder of Dr. Valentine was that the doctor caught the defendant stealing drugs from the Moskowitz medical laboratory. The prior for drug sales is directly related and shows the defendant's state of mind at the time of the crime. Res gestae, Judge."

"Yeah, I think it's res gestae," the judge said, scratching his chin.

"Race what?" Cletus whispered.

"Motion denied!" the judge ruled. "We'll take an hour and a half for lunch. Then, Mr. Snedley, you can begin to call your witnesses."

"But, Your Honor . . ." Tubby pleaded.

"I already ruled," Stifflemire said, on his way out the door.

Cletus looked at Tubby, a frightened expression on his face. "Race what?" he asked again.

"Res gestae. He means your state of mind," Tubby told him.

"Mine's bad," Cletus said.

A deputy sheriff led the disconsolate prisoner away to the courthouse jail downstairs. Tubby collected Cherrylynn, and they walked over to Ditcharo's for a sandwich. Even the cheerful hellos from the ladies behind the counter didn't brighten their mood. Steaming red beans and rice, a shot of hot sauce, some French bread, a nice piece of smoked sausage, and a bowl of bread pudding for after helped a little.

"Golly, I almost forgot." Tubby went to the booth to make a call.

"Hello, Denise? Listen, I'm still in the middle of my trial, but I did talk to your Uncle Roger's lawyer. We've made a lot of progress."

"What's happened?"

"Well, I told him I could prove your stock certificate for a thousand shares was good, and I had the law to back it up. I explained how we would decimate him in court. After quite a bit of argument, he finally offered to split the company fifty-fifty. You would have a thousand shares and so would Uncle Roger."

"That sounds fine."

"Not so fast. Don't forget you have that extra certificate for a hundred shares. We could hold out for control of the company, but Guyoz made it clear they will fight us in court for that."

"I'm willing to forget the hundred shares, Mr. Dubonnet. Roger is still family, and I'll give up a little."

"He also wants to keep getting his salary from the company."

"Tell him that's okay too, but I want the same salary."

"Sure, fine." Tubby liked that. "Guyoz says he wants to settle right away because there's an oil-drilling contract to finalize."

"I'm aware of it. The driller wants to pay us two hundred thousand this year with options for the next six years."

"With that kind of money, you won't have to keep boxing."

"I wouldn't give up boxing if I made a million bucks, Mr. Dubonnet. It's just something I really like to do."

"You may be the richest female fighter in Louisiana."

"Don't forget, I have to pay one quarter to you."

"Oh, yeah," Tubby said—like he would forget that.

"Mr. Dubonnet, thanks for staying in my corner."

"You were vouched for," he said.

"I heard," she said. "Can you come see me at Coconut Casino Saturday night?" Her voice was eager.

"Not unless my murder trial ends tomorrow, and that won't happen unless someone confesses."

"Then I hope they confess."

"The guilty always should," he said. "Listen, I've got a meal on the table. I'll call you when I know something else."

She hung up, and Tubby hurried back to his lunch.

A bearded man wearing a black leather vest and a pound of silver buckles and buttons sat on the wall and played his guitar softly. He was trying out "Mr. Bojangles." He had placed a soft hat on the pavement, begging for change, and pigeons walked around it eating crumbs.

There were not so many tourists today in Spanish Plaza, where Canal Street meets the Mississippi River. Three Japanese couples were shooting photographs of each other by the fountain. Had they looked closely, they would have seen in the background two nicely dressed men leaning on the rail over by the water, deep in conversation.

"Many things in life do not go as we would hope," Mr. Flick was saying. His eyes followed a bright red towboat, radar revolving, churning upstream.

Walter was thinking that Flick's age was showing. He had observed the concern his employer exhibited over those little crevices around his eyes and lips—the care he took to avoid letting the muscles of his face do what they pleased when they tried to express what Flick felt. But whatever creams and tonics the man worked into his flesh had failed him this afternoon. He was revealing some very unattractive tension.

"I have always looked forward to my visits to New Orleans," Flick continued. "It's the sense you get of unreality. Something that is very difficult to induce in Fort Worth."

What's wrong with reality? Walter was thinking. He stood a head taller than Flick. He was keenly aware of his own ability to survive in a world that favored strong, handsome, fast, and smart men.

"It is possible to lose yourself here, and at the same time look for who you are, if you follow."

Walter nodded. He tapped his shoe on the concrete to warn away a pigeon that was pecking about too close.

"And I don't want to let that go, Walter." Flick turned away from the river and looked at the young man. "I cannot bear the thought of losing this."

Walter saw the anger behind Mr. Flick's pale blue eyes, and he felt suddenly nervous.

He kept his voice steady, however, when he said, "I'm not making any excuses. I took the best opportunity that presented itself. It was nothing short of a miracle that the lawyer walked away from the accident. If you had been there you would see I'm right."

Flick shuddered.

"I have no wish ever to be there," he said. "I am deathly afraid that I have already involved myself too deeply. You

may know that my least favorite emotion is fear. It was
your task, Walter, to protect me from fear.''

"I'm sorry if you feel I've let you down," Walter said
earnestly. "I guarantee it won't happen again. I'll take care
of him tonight—simple as that.''

"It's too late," Flick said sharply. "If he gets killed
now, there's bound to be some inquiry. At the very least it
will delay the trial. That's the problem, Walter.'' He spread
out the fingers of his hand and pressed them gently against
Walter's chest, as if he might conjure him over the railing
and into the water.

"We can solve the problem," Walter pleaded, mad at
himself for letting his composure crack.

"Come walk with me," Flick said. He set off, strolling
slowly in the direction of the landing for the ferry to Al-
giers.

"I think that what we must do now is destroy all of the
evidence.''

"You mean in the lab?" Walter asked, trying to follow.

"Exactly," Flick said. "Now put your mind to work
figuring out how to accomplish that.''

A panhandler with burgundy pants and a pink tank top
noticed their approach and came to life to intercept them.

"Betcha I can tell you where you got them shoes.'' He
grinned desperately.

Flick pressed a dollar into the thin hand and brushed past.
Walter gave the man a menacing scowl and a push.

"Well, access to the lab should be no problem," he began as they walked on, leaving the vagrant teetering on
wobbly legs.

"Hush, Walter," Flick interrupted him. "I don't want to
know your plan. Your future with me is determined by your
success, not by the means you employ to achieve it.''

"I understand," Walter said.

"But do it quickly. I cannot tell you what this means to
me.'' The sweep of his hand took in the approaching fer-
ryboat, horn blasting, the seagulls squawking above it; the
Asian children running across the plaza to an ice cream
vendor; the faces in the clouds; two lovers with rings in

their lips telling secrets on a bench. "Please approach this as if your life depended on it."

"Consider it done," Walter said. He wished now he had never gotten mixed up with this crazy old man.

That afternoon the wheels of justice rolled relentlessly on. Clayton Snedley began to deal out his cards. The case of the headless ice man was interesting enough to merit the attention of the parish's chief medical examiner, who so proficiently and methodically described the frozen state of the body and the interesting phenomenon of its head cracking off like an icicle that there was hardly anyplace to go on cross-examination. The jury was entranced. Since Tubby knew the good Dr. Jazz socially, he asked only a couple of perfunctory questions. Their purpose was to let the jury see that the defense counsel was the kind of man who received cordial and respectful treatment from bigwigs like the coroner.

"So the actual cause of death was not the freezing, nor the head falling off. It was a stab wound in the neck, am I right?"

"Yes, that's right, Mr. Dubonnet."

"Which could have been a scalpel."

"A scalpel would certainly fit the bill, yes sir."

It was just for show.

The next witness was the security guard, who told about finding Cletus holding Dr. Valentine's head.

"He looked to me like he was leaving the room with it," guard Josef Malouf testified.

"On the Friday before you found the defendant and the body, were you on duty?" Tubby asked on cross-examination.

"Sure was."

"Did you see Mr. Busters enter the lab?"

"I imagine I did. He worked Fridays."

"But you don't remember really seeing him?"

"Can't say that I do, exactly."

"Who did enter the lab?"

"I didn't keep a list of everyone."

"Isn't it a fact that lots of nurses and doctors and orderlies pass right by your station in the corridor?"

"Yeah, but not so much at night."

"On that Friday, you don't remember who went in and out, do you?"

"Not really."

"Almost anybody outfitted in hospital-type clothing could have passed you without causing you to notice, right?"

"Sure I would notice. That's what I get paid for."

"Do you remember who went in and out or don't you?" Malouf looked uncomfortable. "Not exactly, no."

"Okay, now you said that when you went into the lab on Sunday night and met Mr. Busters, he seemed to be leaving the room."

"You mean when I saw Cletus with Dr. Valentine's head?"

"Yes," Tubby said testily.

"He looked to me like he was leaving the lab with the head."

"Did it occur to you he might be on his way to find you, the security guard?"

Malouf puckered his lips and shook his head violently.

"You have to say your answer, not just move your head," Judge Stifflemire lectured.

"If he was coming to get me, he didn't look very happy when he saw me standing in the doorway."

Tubby used the walk back to the counsel table to compose his face.

"No more questions," he proclaimed triumphantly.

"That was good?" Cletus asked as guard Malouf walked past. Tubby looked at him and crossed his eyes. Then he turned around and smiled at the jury.

"Good as a sharp stick in the eye," he whispered between his teeth.

To nail the coffin, Snedley called Detective Porknoy of the New Orleans Police Department.

chapter 28

The district attorney warmed Porknoy up with a couple of easy questions to establish his impressive credentials as one of the city's foremost crime fighters. Fourteen years on the force. Three in homicide. Porknoy, who never seemed too moved by anything, seemed animated, almost human, when he talked about himself.

He told about how he got a call on Sunday night at 11:03 p.m. about an incident at the Moskowitz—which he pronounced "Mass-kee-witz"—lab. How he and Detective Ike Canteberry had responded, and how they finally found their way into the correct wing of the labyrinth. Joe Malouf was watching the door, and Cletus Busters was inside, sitting quietly on a stool and waiting for them. Right by the doorway, on a trolley cart full of cleaning supplies, was a rather pale and wet-looking human head.

On the floor, approximately twenty-four feet in front of the door, was the body itself.

Having brought Porknoy to his climax, Snedley asked, "Whose body was it?"

"Didn't know at the time," Porknoy said sullenly, provoking a glare from the DA.

"Well, who did you determine it to be?"

"Whitney Valentine, M.D. He was identified by a Dean Auchinschloss, head man of the place."

"Did you notice anything unusual about him?"

"He was frozen solid."

"Objection," Tubby cried.

"Why?" the judge asked.

"He's no doctor. Neither is he a weatherman."

"Oh well, okay, sustained."

"After you found the body, what did you do?" Snedley resumed.

"I had the scene secured and called in the forensics unit. Then I interviewed the defendant."

"Cletus Busters?"

"Yes."

"What did he say?"

"He claimed to have discovered the body by accident," Porknoy said incredulously.

"How did the defendant seem to you?"

"Agitated. Excited."

"Did he give you his version of what happened?"

"Objection," Tubby erupted.

The judge looked curious.

"Improper form of question. The word 'version' suggests the defendant was not telling the truth exactly like it happened."

"I don't think that's improper. I'll permit the question."

"So what was his version, Officer Porknoy?"

"He said he was cleaning up the room. He opened the door to this walk-in freezer, and the body of Dr. Valentine fell out, striking the floor, with the resulting head dismemberment."

The DA chewed on that word. He straightened his tie, walked around in a circle, and cleared his throat. "Did you ask him why he opened the door to the freezer?" he resumed.

"I did."

"What did he say?"

"He stopped answering my questions."

"Did you subsequently run a check to see whether the defendant had a prior arrest record?"

"Objection," Tubby yelled.

"I've already ruled, Mr. Dubonnet, that the prior record is admissible."

"But any prior encounters with the law have absolutely nothing to do with this case and are only intended to paint this man black and suggest to the good people of the jury that one mistake in life condemns you forever," Tubby exclaimed excitedly.

"Objection!" Snedley was waving papers, arms spread wide, pleading. "He's arguing his case—"

"Enough!" the judge bellowed. "Everybody sit down. Mr. Dubonnet's objection is overruled and will not be repeated. No, stand up again. I want to see counsel up at the bench."

Snedley and Tubby approached the judge humbly and craned their necks to hear what he had to say in private.

"What are you doing, Mr. Dubonnet? That issue was already disposed of pretrial."

"I'm just trying to protect the record, Judge," Tubby said seriously.

"Well, there's protecting the record and then there's just jacking off," Stifflemire growled.

"Yes sir." Tubby coughed and, conscious of the jury's eyes on his back, nodded vigorously in agreement.

Dismissed, both lawyers hiked back to their tables. Snedley had a big grin on his face.

The jurors shifted around and exchanged glances. They hoped something good was coming.

"Did you run his record through the computer?" Snedley asked the policeman.

"I did."

"What did you find?"

"The defendant has been convicted of distribution of a controlled substance. He was sentenced to three years, of which he served one year and six months at the P. G. T. Beauregard Correctional Institute in Bogalusa."

His back to the judge, Snedley rolled his eyes for the

jury's benefit. "Did you determine that such drugs were kept in the Moskowitz lab?"

"Objection, leading," Tubby piped up.

"Sustained. Try again, Mr. Snedley."

"Did you search the laboratory, and if so what did you find?"

"A large quantity of controlled substances, including phenobarbital-like substances."

"Oh, sure," Tubby complained. "Now he knows what to say."

"I think he could figure it out for himself," the DA said dryly.

"Get on with it, gentlemen," the judge said.

"Where did you locate these phenobarbital-like substances?" Snedley asked.

"In the freezer."

"That wasn't in the police record," Tubby whispered angrily to Cletus, who just looked back at him, in pain. "You didn't tell me that." Tubby kicked his client in the calf.

"Did you determine whether Cletus Busters had ever had an altercation with Dr. Valentine?" Snedley wanted to know.

"Yes."

"How did you find that out?"

"By talking to his partner, Dr. Randolph Swincter."

"Objection! Pure hearsay."

"Mr. Snedley?" the judge inquired.

"No problem, Judge. We call Dr. Randolph Swincter to the stand."

"Hey." Tubby laughed. "Don't I get a cross-examination here?"

The judge nodded, and Snedley sat down with a glare that said he did not like that rule.

"Detective Porknoy," Tubby began, slowly rising. He rested his hand on the shoulder of Cletus, who flinched. Tubby pulled his hand away quickly. "Wouldn't you be agitated and excited if you had just discovered a dead body and saw the head go rolling around the floor?"

"Objection, irrelevant," Snedley cried out.

"Sustained."

"Okay," Tubby said calmly. "Detective, did you ever point-blank ask Mr. Busters whether he killed Dr. Valentine?"

"Yes, and he denied it."

"He said he didn't do it?"

Behind Tubby's back, Snedley was looking askance at the jury.

"Yes," Porknoy conceded.

"When was the murder committed?"

"On Friday night, near as we can tell."

"Did anyone claim to see Mr. Busters with Dr. Valentine that night?"

"No."

"Did anyone hear a fight?"

"Not that I could discover."

"Did you ever find the weapon?"

"No."

"Did you find Dr. Valentine's blood on any of the defendant's clothing?"

"Not the doctor's blood, no."

"Someone else's?"

"We found some animal blood, which I figured—"

"We don't want to know what you figured," Tubby interrupted quickly. "The jury does the figuring. You did not find any human blood in any way connected with this crime on the defendant or his clothing, did you?"

"No."

"Did you investigate any other suspects in this case?"

"None seriously. Our attention quickly focused on the defendant."

"You never looked elsewhere at all, did you? Not at the wife. Not—"

"Objection," the DA shouted.

"Mr. Dubonnet, that's going too far," the judge admonished.

"Your Honor, my point, which will become obvious when we put on our case, is that there are several others"—

Tubby pivoted and took in the courtroom—"who had a motive to kill Dr. Valentine, far more of a motive than Cletus Busters had, but through shortsightedness the police did nothing to follow up on any of these obvious leads."

"Your Honor," Snedley complained.

"All well and good, when it's your turn, Mr. Dubonnet, but you can't get more from this witness. He already said he focused on Mr. Busters."

"Okay, Your Honor. Mr. Porknoy, you said the freezer compartment contained phenobarbital-like drugs."

"That's right."

"And you suggested Cletus may have killed Dr. Valentine to get the drugs."

"That's right."

"The murder was on a Friday night?"

"Yes."

"And the drugs were still there on Sunday?"

Porknoy hesitated. "Yes . . ." he said, starting to look confused.

"Well, why on earth, Detective, if taking drugs was the motive, would the defendant have stuffed the body in the freezer on Friday and waited all weekend to come back and get the drugs?"

"Who knows what these voodoo doctors will do. Maybe he needed to go home and conjure up a spell."

"What?" Tubby yelled. "Objection to that answer as totally unresponsive."

"Sustained! Officer Porknoy, really. The jury will disregard all that."

"No more questions," Tubby said, returning to the old oak chair beside Cletus.

Porknoy heaved himself off the witness stand and threw Tubby a triumphant grin when he stalked past.

"It's late," the judge announced, checking his watch to confirm that it was four-fifteen. "Mr. Snedley, you can bring on your next witness when we reconvene at nine o'clock tomorrow. The jury may go back to the jury room and collect your belongings. Court is adjourned."

Bonk went the gavel.
"All rise!" the bailiff bellowed.

"Bad day for the good guys," was the postmortem Tubby delivered while they waited for their meals. He had invited Flowers and Cherrylynn to join him for dinner at Franky and Johnny's—a neighborhood restaurant uptown, where the air was light with garlic, cayenne, and tomato sauce— so they could go over the case together, but he didn't really feel like talking.

The waitress had brought the men Dixies, and a Heineken for Cherrylynn, who thought she had taste, and a platter of boiled crawfish for the table, bright red and breathing steam. At the bar a clean-up man gently applied a feather duster to the portrait of the founder. The framed jerseys of Joe Namath and Billy Martin on the wall silently reminded everybody that men who suffer big-time know how to enjoy a good meal. But for Tubby, normally at peace with the world, a positive attitude was hard to find tonight.

"That was terrible, the way that disgusting policeman threw in that bit about voodoo," Cherrylynn said angrily.

"All my fault," Tubby moaned, listlessly sucking a crawfish morsel from its moist peppery tail. He reached for his beer. "I should never have asked Porknoy a question that allowed him to say more than yes or no."

"He was going to say it, no matter what," Flowers opined. "He's that kind of a putz."

The waitress came with a tray and began passing around warm plates. Fried shrimp for Cherrylynn, pork chops and black-eyed peas for Flowers, and a big bowl of fragrant, rich, brown seafood gumbo and rice for Tubby, with a roast beef po-boy on the side, extra gravy.

"I don't see how they can convict him on the little bit of evidence the DA put on today," his secretary said.

"They can surely convict him." Tubby tasted his gumbo and immediately felt its restorative effects. "But I'm revising my opinion. I don't think they can give him the death penalty. The jury will have just a little nagging doubt. Our best angle is still to show that someone else had a motive.''

''Trina, uh, Dr. Tessier and I spent a couple of hours going over Valentine's professional writings,'' Flowers said. ''The man was quite a whiz where strange causes of death are concerned. He was a detective, really. But I didn't see anything that looked the least bit relevant.''

''What about the last project? The one he was working on at the time of his death?''

''Not a trace. Very suspicious, huh?'' Flowers said, and made his eyebrows wiggle. ''Good pork chops,'' he added.

''Extremely suspicious,'' Tubby said, dipping some French bread into his soup. ''Let's concentrate on that.''

''What do you suggest?'' Flowers asked. ''You like these fried green pepper rings?'' he asked Cherrylynn.

She nodded, mouth full.

''We know he had lots of notes,'' Tubby said, ''and probably a written report. Maybe they've all been destroyed, in which case we'll never know what he was doing, but then we're no worse off than we are now. Or else they haven't been destroyed and you have until tomorrow morning to find them.''

''Find them where?''

''Detecting is your job. Keeping you out of jail is mine.''

Cherrylynn looked from one to the other, gave it up, and took a dainty swallow of beer.

''How's your shrimp?'' Tubby asked her.

''Real tasty, Mr. D,'' she said.

''They got a nice peanut butter pie, too,'' Tubby suggested.

The latest family news, recorded on the answering machine at home, was that Harold had absconded with Debbie's television, the pearls she had gotten for her high school graduation, and Christine's jambox. ''I'll have to get her another one if she's going to the beach this summer,'' he thought angrily. No one had heard from Harold for three days.

Some guys with shaved heads had come by Debbie's

apartment asking about Harold, but they left when they
were told the truth—Harold's whereabouts were unknown.

Denise had to use an ice cube and a tissue to stop the flow
of blood from her lower lip. With the tips of her fingers on
the other hand she pushed the buttons on the telephone.
Monique was on another line, so she left a message.

She was still repairing the damage from Baxter's visit
when Monique called back.

Instead of saying hello, Denise just cried into the phone
while Monique kept demanding to know what was wrong.

In a minute or two she calmed down enough to tell Monique the story—the theme of which was that Baxter kept
confusing lovemaking with violence. Her girlfriend ran
through the medical checklist and determined that the in-
juries were minor. Dump the son of a bitch, she ordered.

"Yeah, I know," Denise said. "I think I have trouble
distinguishing between hitting and caring."

"Do you like the taste of blood?" Monique demanded,
intending to be sarcastic.

"No," Denise replied, but she had to think about it.

"There's such a thing as professional help," Monique
told her.

"Did you ever have any?"

"No," Monique admitted. "I left town."

"Well, I don't want to do that."

"You shouldn't have to. Just break it off. If he messes
with you, get Mr. Dubonnet to put a peace bond on him."

"I guess," Denise said, her voice distant.

"I guess, I guess," Monique muttered. She was so mad
she wanted to strangle the girl.

chapter 29

It was not hard to disconnect the regulator on the large propane tank that fueled the gas burners and the specimen crematorium in Laboratory 3. A hundred rats twitched their whiskers and watched the shadowy figure move quickly and carefully around the room, opening the gas jets that released the noxious smell. There came a sudden frightening illumination when the human lit a match and left a candle burning on one of the stainless steel countertops before swiftly opening the freezer closet and exiting through the sliding door.

Flowers walked across the front lobby of the medical center unaccosted. The information desk had been abandoned for the night, and Flowers had watched the security guard take a stroll outside to smoke a cigarette. The place smelled like lemon disinfectant. The detective made it past the elevators, where a tired nurse was leaning against the buttons with her eyes closed. He took a right at a sign that said HOSPITAL PERSONNEL ONLY. A page for "Dr. Smith . . . Dr. Merrick, you are wanted . . ." echoed down the empty hall.

The security desk at the approach to Moskowitz lab was vacant, but a cardboard cup of vending machine coffee steamed beside a sign-in log.

Cautiously, Flowers peered around the corner. He could see the security guard at the far end of the hallway. It was not Joe Malouf. The guard was looking with curiosity at the door of Lab 3. He put his hand on the plate that made it open.

With a roar like a cannon discharging, the door of Lab 3 blew out. A ball of green and yellow flame raced down the hall in Flowers's direction. He was thrown back against the wall, and his head cracked hard on the tile floor. Pumping adrenaline, he scrambled back onto his feet. A quick look told him that the guard had disappeared beneath a pile of rubble and the dust and smoke that filled the hall. Flowers could feel the rain of the overhead sprinkler system but he could not hear the alarms, since his ears were not functioning. He stumbled toward a red Emergency Exit sign.

At that moment Tubby was standing on a cracked sidewalk, trying to decide which one of a block-long row of shotgun houses he was supposed to go into. The one directly in front of him seemed to be the right decision, so he climbed up the steps and pulled open one of the green-shuttered doors.

Now the question was what room to pick. The living room was empty but for a television set loudly advertising a medicine for colds. The dining room beyond contained a table set for four. The main course sizzled on each plate, but Tubby couldn't recognize the dish. No, he gagged, it was grilled rat!

He ran into the bedroom and into the arms of two doctors, stethoscopes swinging like live things from around their necks. They tried to wrestle him to the floor.

"Orderlies! Need help!" one cried out.

Tubby broke free and careened back through the house to the street. He jumped into the getaway car and zoomed away. Happily, he realized that it was being driven by Nicole Normande, an old flame. With a smile that had always grabbed his heart, she asked, "Want to come inside for a beer? You need to rest."

The telephone woke him up. Breathing hard, Tubby picked up the handset.

"Hello," he grunted.

"This is Flowers. Moskowitz lab just blew up."

"Say it again," Tubby demanded, struggling for consciousness.

"It blew up. I was close by. I think at least one man got seriously injured—most likely killed."

"Where are you now?"

"I'm at a pay phone on Claiborne Avenue. I got out of the area quick. I figured with so many doctors around, there was no need for one not very straight private investigator. Nobody saw me there."

"Any idea what caused it?"

"Looked like a gas explosion. There was a big fireball. My eyebrows are gone."

"Christ, what about all the animals?"

"They might just be out of their misery."

"I guess we'll learn more on the morning news. Can you stay out of trouble till then?"

"I'll sure try. You know where Grits Bar is?"

"Of course," Tubby said.

"If you need me, I'm on my way over there to get a beer and clean up. And establish an alibi."

"Okay," Tubby said, "but I'm going back to sleep."

He did, but only after tossing around for an hour trying to turn off his brain.

chapter 30

Day two of State versus Busters began just like day one except, alert to Judge Stifflemire's timetable, no one showed up until nine-thirty. Also, it had clouded up overnight and rain was coming down in torrents. Tubby didn't feel like parking the Lincoln and wading through puddles, so he took a cab to the courthouse. Cherrylynn remained at the office to return yesterday's calls and explain that Mr. Dubonnet was in trial. After that she could come to court and watch.

The news media, excited by the explosion at Moskowitz lab, and titillated by the connection to the headless man, were out in force. Tubby brushed past them. For once he had nothing to say. There was a crowd of spectators outside the courtroom, too. A tall man he couldn't place smiled and said hello to him. There was something familiar about the guy, maybe the overpowering cologne he was wearing, but Tubby had big problems on his mind, and he breezed by.

He was just peeling off his overcoat when the judge took the bench with a swirl of his bombazine robe.

The district attorney must have made impressive threats to Dr. Swincter about what could happen if you ignored a subpoena, because despite the turmoil at Moskowitz lab, he popped right up when Clayton Snedley called his name.

Cletus was in a somber funk and barely reacted to Tubby's good morning and words of comradeship. He even turned his head away when Swincter walked by. Tubby whispered that he should sit up straight for the jury, but Cletus ignored him. Bad sign.

Swincter promised to tell the truth, the whole truth, and nothing but the truth, so help him God, and then gave an exposition of his very impressive credentials.

He had known Dr. Valentine for three years, and they had worked together on many important research projects that had expanded the boundaries of medical science. Dr. Valentine had been a useful and innovative scientist, and his loss would be felt deeply by the entire medical community.

"Did Dr. Valentine and Cletus Busters get along?" Snedley inquired.

"No, they didn't. Whitney, uh, Dr. Valentine caught Busters letting research animals out of their cages on one occasion. An experiment was prejudiced thereby. They had quite an argument about it, and I believe Whitney tried to have Cletus fired for it."

"Did you witness the argument?"

"Yes, I did."

"Did the defendant say anything to Dr. Valentine?"

"He called Valentine a name which I took to be 'blasphemer.' I wasn't completely sure because Cletus doesn't speak that well." Swincter gave a little sanctimonious snort and took off his glasses to polish them on his shirt.

"Did Valentine tell you anything else about Cletus?"

"Objection, hearsay," Tubby interrupted.

"Excited utterance, Your Honor. The statement was made by Dr. Valentine during a heated argument with the defendant."

"Overruled. You may answer the question." Snedley turned toward the jury and nodded vigorously in agreement.

"Whitney accused Cletus of taking drugs from the lab. You see, some items had turned up missing." Swincter put his glasses back on his nose.

"What in particular?"

"Phenobarbital."

"No more questions," the DA said.

"No questions for Dr. Swincter on cross-examination, Your Honor." Tubby felt Cletus straighten up next to him. "I do however plan to call him as a witness for the defense on direct."

"Very well. You may step down, Dr. Swincter, but you remain under subpoena."

Swincter made no effort to conceal his irritation as he left the stand.

"That's the state's case, Your Honor. We rest."

And before you could say "Have mercy," Judge Stifflemire had asked whether the defense was ready to commence.

"Yes sir," Tubby responded robustly, but that was not how he felt. This trial was moving much too quickly. And where the hell was Mickey O'Rourke? Couldn't he at least lend some moral support? Rarely had he had such a feeling that his quiver was so empty.

Tubby turned around to survey the prospects again and saw Cherrylynn enter the courtroom. She waved encouragingly and sat down near the back. The grieving widow, chiropractor Bennett, and Magenta Reilly all glared at him from their lairs here and there. Dr. Auchinschloss was chewing his nails.

Mentally, Tubby flipped a coin. "As its first witness, the defense calls Mrs. Ruby Valentine," he announced.

The widow, dressed in a tight cobalt-blue suit with gold buttons, rose and walked down the aisle. She moved with dignity, nodding demurely at the judge as she approached the witness box.

"Mrs. Valentine, my sympathies on your loss," Tubby began.

She just stared at him coldly and did not respond.

"Yes, ahem. Mrs. Valentine, how long were you and your husband married?"

"More than two years."

"You were a nurse when you met him, right?"

"I still am."

"At Moskowitz?"

"No, at St. Doloroso General."

"Did you ever go into Moskowitz lab?"

"I used to, occasionally."

"To see your husband?"

"That's right."

"Did you have to ask directions to find his workplace?"

"No, I knew my way around."

"Right," Tubby said, smiling at the jury. "Mrs. Valentine, would you say you and your husband were happily married?"

"Objection!" Snedley cried indignantly.

"What's your purpose, Mr. Dubonnet?" the judge asked.

"To show other possible motives to kill the decedent."

"I didn't kill my husband," Mrs. Valentine wailed, and began sobbing uncontrollably.

"Mrs. Valentine, please," the judge comforted. He frowned at Tubby and shook his head. "Take a minute to compose yourself."

She kept crying.

Tubby stared at the wall above her head and then dared to glance at the jury. He saw disapproval written on their faces. Quickly looking away, he saw Mickey O'Rourke slipping in the door and sliding onto the back bench beside Cherrylynn.

"Mrs. Valentine," Tubby resumed when she gasped for air, "who is Ira Bennett?"

Boo hoo, boo hoo, the witness continued.

In for a penny, in for a pound, Tubby told himself.

"Isn't it true that you and Ira Bennett had an affair that was going on at the time of your husband's death—and is still ongoing?"

"Yes, you vile man, but I didn't kill Whitney. I loved him. He was just a hopeless philanderer," Mrs. Valentine shrieked.

"Your Honor," both lawyers were yelling at the same time.

The jury, thinking she had described the victim of a terrifying blood disease, grumbled among themselves.

Stifflemire pounded his gavel until everybody shut up.

Tubby saw Magenta run out of the back of the courtroom. He sank down beside Cletus, who was staring at him in disbelief.

"No further questions," he said, exhausted.

"None here," District Attorney Snedley agreed.

"Five-minute recess," Stifflemire announced. "Bailiff, help Mrs. Valentine back to her seat."

"I want to testify," Cletus hissed in Tubby's ear.

"It's a bad idea," the lawyer whispered wearily. "We've talked about this already."

"I got a right. You ain't doin' shit. These people gonna hang me."

"We'll see, Cletus. Just sit tight and let me get my thoughts together." He turned around and waved at Mickey O'Rourke to come up. Reluctantly, Mickey arose and began to shuffle slowly forward. He looked at the chair beside Tubby like it might be full of snakes.

"Counsel table, Mickey. You've been here before."

Mickey laughed, like it hurt him.

"You sober?" Tubby asked.

"Way too sober," Mickey answered.

"Well, you might as well take a witness. You can't do any worse than me."

"Wanna bet?"

"You saw that jury, Mickey. I've alienated at least half of them. You have to make them forgive me."

"How?" Mickey pleaded.

"You'll do it. Just be yourself," Tubby said encouragingly. "Juries pick up on things. If you stumble a little bit, they'll probably sympathize. They may even figure out why. I really think you can help us, Mickey. Don't you, Cletus?"

Cletus was watching them both in horror. Tubby grinned back. "Just kidding, Cletus," he said.

"You're nuttier than I am," Busters moaned.

"No doubt. Here come de judge."

Stifflemire took the bench and let everybody sit down again.

"I see Mr. O'Rourke has joined us," he said, peering over his spectacles.

"Yes, Your Honor. My co-counsel will call the next witness. If I may just have a moment, Judge."

The judge told him to take two.

"I think you should call Bennett, the chiropractor," Tubby whispered. "Just ask him about his affair with Mrs. Valentine. He's such a jerk, he'll make Cletus seem like an angel by comparison. Who knows, you might get lucky and he'll confess."

Mickey looked over his shoulder. "You mean the guy in the third row?" he asked.

"Yeah, that's him."

Bennett, all 210 pounds of him, was scowling at the defense, breathing heavily like a bull anxious to crash out of the chutes.

"No way," Mickey said.

"What do you mean, no way?"

"He's too hostile."

"For Christ's sake, Mickey."

"My doctor told me to avoid conflict, Tubby. That's how I'm going to get sober. I'm staying serene."

"Ah, man." Tubby rubbed his forehead.

"About ready, counselors?" the judge asked.

"Almost, Judge," Tubby said. His eyes roamed the room. Magenta hadn't come back. Cross her off the list. "Well, look. How about Dr. Swincter? He's smooth as ten-year-old Scotch, I mean owl shit. Ask him about his research with the deceased. Lead up to that last project. Let's see what we learn."

"Okay, I guess," Mickey said. He fumbled with the knot in his wrinkled Tabasco tie.

"Well, call the witness for Christ's sake."

O'Rourke stood up shakily and held on to his chair with both hands.

"Defense calls Dr. John Swincter," he said in a low voice.

"Randolph Swincter," Tubby prompted.

"Randolph," O'Rourke corrected himself.

"Maybe he'll get into the swing of it as he goes along," Tubby whispered to Cletus. "He's been a top lawyer in his time."

Cletus was not responding.

Swincter came forward again and composed himself in the witness box. He pursed his lips and looked disdainfully upon the defense team.

"Dr. Swincter," Mickey began, "tell me a little about the research you and Dr. Valentine did together."

"Surely," Swincter said with confidence, turning toward the jury. "The purpose of our work has been disease, its roots, its causes, and . . ."

Tubby tuned out. Songs began running through his mind. His fingers began drumming on the table. Cletus nudged him. Oh, what? Jesus, where to go from here?

"What are we doing?" Cletus hissed.

I didn't go to law school, Tubby told himself. I'm really a tugboat captain. So hard to be an honest man in a chaotic world. Now where did I pick that up? He remembered vaguely where he was and nodded, reassuringly he hoped, to Cletus.

"What project were you working on at the time of Dr. Valentine's death?" he heard Mickey inquire.

"Pinpointing the edema that reacts to protyestran . . ." Swincter discoursed on.

A hand grabbed Tubby's shoulder and shook it. He jerked around, thinking it was that pesky client of his again, but he beheld Flowers's excited face on the other side of the rail. He thrust a thick manuscript of some kind, fastened with a blue spiral binder, into Tubby's hands.

"Found it in Swincter's microwave," he whispered to Tubby.

Tubby stared at what he held in his hands. The title glowed through its clear plastic cover: "Cardiac Toxicity of Endflu as the Cause of Two Deaths."

What the heck is this? Tubby asked himself. He looked up and found Mickey standing over him in distress.

"I've run out of questions," he confided to Tubby.

"Ask him what this is," Tubby suggested.

O'Rourke took the document and looked it over curiously. Then he spun around and raised the manuscript high in the air above his head.

"Dr. Swincter," he demanded, "what the heck is this?"

Swincter put his hands out as if to ward off a blow.

Then he covered his face with them and began sobbing. O'Rourke jumped back to the counsel table.

"What did I do?" he screeched at Tubby in confusion.

"It was in the microwave," Tubby prompted desperately.

"Your Honor," O'Rourke blundered on. "We have reason to believe Dr. Swincter was endeavoring to microwave this, um, document."

Judge Stifflemire looked puzzled but intrigued.

"So continue," he suggested, over Swincter's moaning.

"Yes, Your Honor. And the question is, I repeat, what the heck is this?"

Swincter's sobs turned to shrieks of laughter. He faced the jury.

"Microwave? Microwave? Why didn't I burn it like they've burned my lab? It's the inquiring scientific mind, you see. So what would you have done? My God, I'm not a monster." Swincter blew his nose. "Stupid, yes, but I assure you they made me do it."

Who made him do what? groped Tubby, his mind no longer razor-sharp. In the courtroom stunned perplexity; then cries of "W'uz up?" and "No way!" rocked the hall. Pandemonium reigned.

chapter **31**

The hastily organized celebration that afternoon was at Mike's Bar. The defense was all accounted for, as well as Raisin Partlow and Trina Tessier, both of whom Tubby had enthusiastically telephoned as soon as the jury was discharged. And as soon as he had made a triumphant speech to the reporters crowded on the majestic courthouse steps. The rain had stopped and the sun was out, giving the cameras a perfect light for the evening news. Tubby had even invited Denise DiMaggio, but she said she was stuck at Swan's Gym. He suggested maybe he would come grab her for dinner later and they could celebrate her victory over her uncle. Inside, he wanted to make amends for suspecting her of being a bad client. Denise said that would be just great.

"Barqs all around," Tubby yelled in deference to Mickey's shot at sobriety.

"Make mine a Tequila Sunrise," Cherrylynn shouted out, and ignored Tubby's reproachful look.

"I don't think I've quite got it figured out," Mickey admitted.

"Shhh," Tubby whispered. "Never let anyone hear you say that." He hoisted his glass.

"A toast to Mickey F. Lee Nizer Johnnie Cochran O'Rourke," he proclaimed.

"Hear hear." Flowers joined in. "And his masterful trick question: What the heck is this?"

They drank. Fats Domino came on the jukebox and started his sly walk up Blueberry Hill.

"What the heck was it, Mickey?" Raisin Partlow asked, having a little bit of a mean streak.

"Allow me to explain," Tubby interjected diplomatically. "Having received the district attorney's personal apologies, I can fill you in with the greatest detail."

"Please do," Raisin said. "Bartender, make my Barq's a bourbon and water."

"The mystery report, which fell into our hands courtesy of the skill of Sanré Fueres, revealed a connection between Endflu, which everyone knows is an extremely popular cold medicine, and Mascatell, a drug I never heard of but that many women take for menstrual pain. Taken together, the two drugs can cause a change in the rhythm of the heart that might result in unconsciousness or permanent damage. Valentine, with Swincter's help, discovered that this was the cause of death of Mrs. Wascomb, who wrecked her car on Lake Pontchartrain, and also the lady from Texas who died in the taxicab."

"I've taken Mascatell," Cherrylynn said, aghast.

"Lots of women do," Tubby said. "Lucky you never had a cold at the same time. No telling how many people may have died or had a severe reaction to it. The rumor at this point is that the people who manufacture Endflu learned about the research—maybe from Swincter or Valentine or, who knows, even Auchinschloss—and paid a visit to the lab. They tried to put a lid on the research, probably by offering money. This would explain Swincter's bank account. It seems Valentine refused to bury his research, so they killed him. Cold, huh? The police were still interrogating Swincter when I left, so I don't know the whole story yet."

"Dr. Valentine was a brave man," Cherrylynn said.

"Not so brave," Trina Tessier said. "As I read the report, there is a simple modification of the Endflu formula that renders it harmless when taken with Mascatell. Except for one small problem, Petroflex Pharmaceuticals could have easily corrected the product.''

"What was the problem?" Cherrylyn asked.

"Dr. Valentine had patented the improved drug. He very likely was going to charge the Endflu people a hefty royalty for using it.''

"That patent should really belong to Moskowitz lab, Valentine's employer,'' Tubby pointed out.

"I couldn't agree more, counselor,'' Tessier said. "We're certainly not going to let Ruby Valentine get rich. I'm going to suggest to Dean Auchinschloss that the school retain you to get that patent back for us. As the senior researcher now, I expect my recommendation will carry some weight. That patent could literally be worth billions of dollars.''

"I'll certainly do my best to help,'' Tubby said immediately.

"Phone call for Dr. Tessier,'' Larry intoned from the bar.

"Damn!'' Trina exclaimed. "Excuse me, but I'm on call. Somebody probably needs a liver section.'' She got up and crossed the room to the wooden telephone booth.

"She's sure a hardworking lady,'' Tubby said, watching her leave. He was fond of new clients who promised to pay him.

"Who did the actual murder?'' Cherrylynn wanted to know.

"The police think Swincter did,'' Tubby said. "But he may have had an accomplice at Endflu.''

"Did I mention,'' Flowers said in a low voice for Tubby's ears, "that when I went over to Swincter's house I saw Trina coming out of the back door?''

"Before you found the report in the kitchen?'' Tubby asked, frowning.

"Yeah.''

"Where's Cletus?'' Cherrylynn asked.

"He's out of jail,'' Mickey said. "He told me he just

wanted to go home. He also said we should beware—the full story hasn't been told.''

''I wish you had brought him over here,'' Tubby said.

''I tried,'' Mickey explained. ''But he said Mr. Dubonnet is a lunatic.''

''Really?'' Tubby asked, trying not to look crestfallen.

''I'm afraid so, Tubby. But he also said I was a drunk.''

''Go figure,'' Raisin said.

Trina came back with a happy expression.

''I don't have to go,'' she said. ''It was just Dean Auchinschloss with some news. Dr. Swincter had some kind of stroke or seizure at the police station. He's in a coma. They took him to New Orleans General.''

''Did he confess to the murder?''

''Not quite,'' Tessier said. ''He mentioned Oscar Flick, who runs the regional Petroflex office. He's been around for years, and I can't believe he's involved in anything like that. Swincter claims the actual murder was committed by some guy he calls 'Walter' who he says worked for Flick.

''Funny thing,'' Tessier continued, ''Swincter even tried to pin something on me. The twerp told the police that I knew this Walter and could identify him too. He's either lying or very confused. I certainly don't remember meeting any Walter.''

''When does Swincter say you met him?'' Tubby asked.

''Wait. He says you met him too, Tubby—the first day you came to the lab. Do you remember meeting any man there?''

A memory of strong cologne passed through Tubby's mind. He recalled a tall man in the hallway, a man he might have seen in the courtroom this very morning.

''Hey, maybe I'm a witness,'' he told the table. ''Ain't that a kick.''

''If Swincter doesn't wake up, you may be the only witness,'' Flowers remarked.

No one could think of a snappy comeback to that.

''Well, that's no reason to stop the party,'' Tubby declared.

"Whaddya say we drink to your health?" Mickey asked the table.

Tubby tapped Dr. Tessier's elbow.

"I guess if you had had Dr. Valentine's research, you would have been in a position to extort a lot of money from Petroflex." His expression was innocent.

"I'm just happy being the head of the laboratory," she replied sweetly. Hers was, too.

Larry brought another round, and good spirits prevailed.

But the feelings were not universal. Walter had at that moment been directed to bail out by Mr. Flick. Just leave town, his boss had ordered. Walter, in his embarrassment, had started to apologize for the whole thing, though it had not been his fault at all.

Flick had cut him off.

"Enough for now," Flick had said. "We will discuss the details of what happened, and your future, later."

After Flick hung up on him Walter rubbed his eyes and suppressed a scream. He beat the plastic receiver against the pay phone until he noticed the people at the bus stop staring at him. He walked away quickly, leaving the cracked handset dangling from its steel cable. It was no longer a question of strategy. It was now a simple matter of pride and professional revenge.

chapter **32**

It was a few minutes past six o'clock when the party at Mike's broke up. Tubby waved goodbye to Mickey O'Rourke, who, wisely, had called a United Cab. Cherrylynn, who had arrived with Tubby, departed with Flowers. Her boss decided to think about that in the morning. He was a little loaded, to tell the truth. On the sidewalk he yielded the right of way to a lopsided bicycle full of kids. The one on the handlebars' job was to go "beep beep," and the lawyer stepped off the curb into the street where old beads and glass fragments sparkled. As an afterthought he beeped back at them.

He had invited Trina Tessier to join him and Denise for dinner, but she said she had work to do. After seeing the doctor safely to her car, he pointed his own downtown.

On a whim, he stopped at a cigar store near Lee Circle and picked up a celebration Partagas that cost about four bucks.

Tubby finally found a safe-looking parking place two blocks from Swan's Gym on Clio Street in front of a neat white house where an elderly lady rocked gently on the porch. Exchanging hellos with her, he locked up and started walking down the sidewalk, without noticing the blue Ford Taurus that pulled to the curb across the street. Over the gym's front door there was a neatly painted picture of a swan—nothing mean and nothing fancy. It did not look like a place where people got bruised.

The sounds that greeted him once inside, however, were the grunts of exertion, thumps on punching bags, and loud derisive comments that echoed off the high ceiling. The smells were leather, floor wax, and sweat. Boxers were at work under the lights in two rings, and men and women in gray or red Ringside sweat suits pounded it out on exercise machines whose functions Tubby did not try to grasp.

He had left his suit coat in the car so that he might look a little less conspicuous, but hell, he was a lawyer, so he kept on his tie.

He saw Baxter Sharpe, Denise's trainer, who waved him away and pointed toward the far corner. Tubby saw a tornado in a sparring helmet beating the dust off a punching bag. He wasn't certain it was Denise until he got close enough for her to notice him and smile.

"Hiya," she said cheerfully, and gave the bag a smack for punctuation.

"You're smoking that thing," Tubby commented. He gave it a sock, and it hurt his knuckles.

"You want to go a few rounds?" Denise asked, and jabbed a couple in his direction.

"No, no." He took a step backwards. "Pick on somebody your own size. I'm just here to take you out to eat."

"I'm almost done here," Denise promised. "Give me time to shower. I'm quick."

Tubby found a bench from which he could watch two brown-skinned boys whale the tar out of each other, as his father used to say, in the ring. Their coach jumped through the ropes and told them to take it easy, so they slowed their pace to awkward poking. They looked about fifteen years old to Tubby, but he was always way off. He looked around for his formerly potential client, Denise's coach, but now he didn't see him.

"Ready." Her announcement surprised him.

Tubby followed her out of the gym, enjoying the scent of her shampoo and trying to remember her age.

"Where are we headed?" she asked outside. The street was dark.

"It's up to you. My car is down the street. There's a pretty good steak restaurant a few blocks from here. You ever been to Doug's Place? I took my daughters there and they loved it." His girls had really liked the spacious airy feeling, all the light wood, and the "primitive" art that adorned the walls of the restored recording studio. Tubby thought it amazing that simple scenes of the "Old South" were now so popular with urban young people who had never so much as seen a real cotton boll. Scary that what to him was just a routine part of growing up in the hot and flat part of Dixie was now exotic. His daughters had seemed to feel that steaks served in such an artsy place were actually good for you, which was fine with him.

"I don't eat meat," Denise said apologetically. "And I'm supposed to be in training for my big fight. If you wouldn't mind a little drive, I know a real nice vegetarian place on Esplanade. Or how about sushi?"

Gad. "How about some oysters?" he suggested hopefully, and began piloting her along the sidewalk toward his car.

He never got an answer. A large man with a woman's stocking pulled over his head stepped out of the shadows between two buildings and blocked their way. He rammed a handgun into Tubby's chest so hard that it knocked him backwards.

"Give me your money, asshole," he demanded urgently. His features were hidden, but Tubby couldn't miss the smell of Purple Musk.

"Damn right," Tubby shouted, hands in the air. "I'm getting my wallet. I want you to have it." He lowered his arm and reached slowly behind him for his pants pocket.

"Speed it up, turkey," the robber grunted, and whapped the pistol against the side of Tubby's head.

Tubby tried to block the blow and his fingers got smacked against his forehead so hard that he felt intense pain in two extremities at once. Part of him lunged for the weapon and part of him focused on the black barrel hole an inch from his nose.

Then the hole jerked away. A fist streaked from the right and caught the assailant square in the mouth.

His lips split into a new grin, and a moist red spot appeared on the pantyhose mask.

"Biff," he said.

Denise caught him with two left jabs in the eyes and another that popped his nose with another splash of blood.

The man stumbled backwards, swaying with the gun, but Denise was close upon him, working on his abdomen and his nose some more.

Tubby observed this from a crouch, his hand to his cheek. Finally he made himself move and jump for the pistol. The floating arm eluded his grasp and the butt of the weapon connected with his forehead.

Tubby saw stars and dizzily renewed his crouch, on one knee.

He was slightly aware that the gun, a nasty-looking Colt automatic, had come loose and was lying on the curb. Meanwhile, Denise was continuing to go whack, whack.

"Uh, biff," the man said, spinnning around twice.

Denise was in heaven. Something black and ugly in her brain was getting a whipping, and her heart was light.

"Yay!" she yelled, socking the man in the kidneys.

He grunted in pain, and, bent over at the waist, he turned and ran away from her down the street. He was trailing blood and moving fast, if unevenly.

Denise, panting, watched him go. She sucked up a deep breath and sparred in the air. Cheers of a phantom crowd rang in her ears. She trotted back to check on Tubby.

"Are you all right?" she sang.

"Your hands must be broken," he wheezed, trying to straighten up.

"This one could be," she said happily, inspecting the fingers on her right. "It hurts like hell." Her knuckles were bleeding.

"God, you were great," Tubby said while he tenderly touched different spots on his head.

"So were you."

"Baloney. Look, you want sushi, you got sushi."

"Oysters would be okay," she said with a smile, as she helped Tubby to the car.

He was thinking that he needed lots of oysters, like a steady diet. She was thinking that she might have put herself out of commission for her upcoming bout, but who cared.

"We'll call the police from the restaurant," he proposed.

"Whatever," she said. She was still skipping around the ring.

Walter was scrambling down the steep stairs of the Pontalba Building, canvas flight bag in hand, when he met Lieutenant Porknoy and two uniformed policemen coming up.

"Going on a trip?" Porknoy asked, tapping the man on his chest.

"Yes, I have a plane to catch. What's the problem?"

"Upstairs, you. I have a warrant for Oscar Flick."

Mr. Flick welcomed the arrival of the police with an offer of wine.

Porknoy declined.

"Are you Oscar Flick?" he demanded.

"I am. Won't you gentlemen sit down?"

"I have a warrant for your arrest in the murder of Dr. Whitney Valentine."

Flick did not look surprised. Neither did he look happy. His eyes searched the room, but the uniforms had walked around to block the French doors, and Porknoy was in front of him.

"Who is this fellow?" Porknoy wanted to know.

"This is a neighbor of mine," Flick said quickly. Walter still had his flight bag in his hand.

"A neighbor, huh?" Porknoy commented suspiciously. He stepped up to Walter, his nose to the tall man's chin.

"I see you got a black eye," the detective observed.

"I tripped and fell—on the pavement in Jackson Square."

"You got a cut lip, too," Porknoy pointed out.

"I hit the sidewalk hard," Walter explained.

"You fit the description of a fella assaulted a young lady and a lawyer named Tubby Dubonnet outside of Swan's Gym," Porknoy insisted.

"Wasn't me, Officer. I was here with my friend playing chess."

Porknoy considered this while he scratched his chin. Then he smiled.

"That being the case," he said, "you can go. Our warrant is for Oscar Flick, and that's you, is it not?" He turned to face the older man.

"I'm afraid it is."

"Okay. Get your things."

"Can I take a toothbrush?" Flick asked, as his partner hustled downstairs and out into the night.

"Absolutely," Porknoy said.

Flick went into the regal bath to collect his shaving kit. Quickly, he extracted a plastic bottle from the medicine cabinet, popped it, and swallowed three capsules.

It would make the ordeal ahead avoidable, entirely avoidable.

chapter 33

Mississippi's Coconut Casino is only an hour and twenty minutes from New Orleans, and it has a parking lot the size of the one at the Superdome.

"Look at all the Louisiana tags," Raisin said, while he navigated Tubby's Lincoln into a space about half a mile from the main entrance. "No wonder our state is broke all the time."

"Maybe they just have crowds like this on fight nights," Tubby said.

"Ladies' boxing is not exactly Mike Tyson," Raisin commented.

"It's going to be a real crowd pleaser someday," Tubby said. "Just wait till they get a look at my girl Denise. This is the sport of the future."

They set off hiking toward the distant lights.

They were not alone. By the time they reached the front door they were part of a steadily flowing crowd of snow-birds from Canada, Airstream campers, New Orleans tour-bus groupies with go-cups, a few barge pilots, and quite a few lads and lassies wearing cowboy hats and boots, fresh from the day shift. Inside it was well lit and well ventilated. The crowd split, half going toward the gaming floor on the other side of a white line painted on the floor. This marked the hypothetical shoreline, the divide between that part of Mississippi earth where gambling was prohibited and the water flowing beneath their feet, where games of chance were encouraged.

The other half of the crowd, with Raisin and Tubby along, went upstairs to the gateway of the boxing arena.

"Quite a place," Tubby shouted, over the din of slot machine bells and whistles and the general mirth of gamblers consuming free drinks.

"I'd like to have the No-Doz concession here," Raisin replied.

The boxing arena was smaller than Tubby expected, but a far cry from the cigar smoke–filled gymnasium he had imagined. It was all new, brightly lit, and the seats were upholstered a garish Mardi Gras purple.

"This ain't the Army, dude," he yelled at Raisin, who gave him the high sign.

They were ushered into their seats by a lovely young girl wearing blue tights showered in sequins. When she moved, the eyes of the fans moved with her.

The program said the headliner was a light heavyweight bout between Zitty Garcia and Montana Denver, but that would come later. First there was the warm-up match they had come to see—an exhibition between "New Orleans's Own Denise DiMaggio" and Roseanne Spratt of Nashville, Tennessee.

Raisin got them a couple of beers, and they settled down with their programs.

"How's the kids?" Raisin asked to make conversation.

"They're doing fine." Tubby had not yet decided to tell anyone about Debbie's pregnancy. "Except that Mattie's no-good brother, Harold, ripped off Debbie's apartment. He's always into something. And I haven't the faintest idea what Christine's up to. She says her grades are fine, but she hasn't sent off her college applications yet. Now, Collette"—he allowed himself to glow—"is the world's primo fifteen-year-old. You know she's been getting me to take her to church?"

"Really. Are you going tomorrow morning?"

"Uh, probably not." Found guilty again.

"Do they have any idea what you do for a living, old buddy?" Raisin asked.

"That's a deep question, man. I don't even have much of a grasp on that one myself."

"I just wondered if they ever came to see you in court."

"At one time or another, all of them have had that pleasure. I've tried to arrange it so that the occasions have been arguments to the Court of Appeal, when I am at my lawyerly best. I've never invited anyone to watch me at a trial."

"It would make you nervous?"

"It might embarrass me, is the real reason."

"I thought you were a great trial lawyer."

"Who told you that?"

"You did."

"It would be more truthful to say I'm a seasoned lawyer."

"What's 'seasoned' mean?"

"That means I've had my ass kicked a few times."

A bell sounded loudly and the ring announcer proclaimed that the first bout, between "two lady sportsmen," was about to begin.

Loud cheers and whistles, Tubby's included, greeted Denise as she paraded down the ramp from her dressing room. She was decked out in a yellow silk robe. When she climbed over the ropes and into the ring she stripped it off, to more ovation, revealing her multicolored tights. The crowd expressed its appreciation.

Roseanne from Nashville got much the same reception. Raisin remarked that she had the largest chest he had ever seen on an athlete.

Both fighters pranced around the ring, sparring in the air and nodding at the advice from their trainers. He waved at Denise, and gustily added his support, but she didn't pick him out. He noticed that her ringside coach was not Baxter Sharpe.

The referee gave the fighters their instructions in the center of the ring and sent them back to their corners.

The gong rang, and both women came out hopping. They circled around each other warily, and then Denise stepped in with some quick left jabs.

Roseanne ducked and bobbed away. Denise followed, and suddenly they were both flailing away at each other. The crowd loved it. And what was not to love? Hard female bodies, nice curves, taut muscles, faces straining in exertion.

Denise's head jerked back when a roundhouse right got under her ear, but she recovered and closed up with her opponent. She was pounding Roseanne's stomach when the bell rang to end the first round.

Both women went back to their corners and flopped down to let their attendants clean them up.

Tubby felt sick.

"I don't know what's wrong with me," he mumbled to Raisin, "but something is making me feel bad. I need to get out of here for a minute."

"You gonna be okay?" Raisin asked, concerned.

"Just need a little air," Tubby said. "You stay here. Tell me how it comes out. I'll be right downstairs."

He made his way over the knees of the cheering fans and stumbled toward the exit. He heard the bell signal the start of the second round as he banged through the swinging doors. His head was swirling a little, but it was his stomach he was worried about. Something about seeing Denise slugged on the face had gotten to him.

He went to the men's room, where lots of other groggy-looking patrons were splashing water on themselves at a score of sinks lined up in a row. Tubby found his place and followed suit. Apparently ladies' professional boxing was not the sport for him.

"I just won three thousand bucks!" the guy at the next sink with the House of Blues T-shirt spread over his world-class beer belly ranted.

"Great," Tubby gurgled between his fingers.

"I just won three thousand bucks," the guy said over his other shoulder.

"I suggest you get out while you can," the next man facing the wall advised.

"I just . . ."

Tubby left. Outside in the lobby he felt better. He strolled toward the gaming floor, past the buffet dining area where great flanks of roast beef were being carved up for gamblers in polo shirts and blue jeans.

"Hello, Tubby," a familiar voice said softly.

He turned and found Nicole Normande seated with a lanky cowboy at one of the oval tables.

"Hello, Nicole," he managed to say.

"You don't look very happy to see me." She was an old girlfriend, sort of. At least they had spent a sunny morning fishing together.

"A blast from the past," he commented. "I thought you were out West."

"I'm back for a while. I'm sorry. Geraldo, this is Tubby Dubonnet. He's a lawyer."

"Pleased to meet you," Geraldo said. He tapped the brim of his Garth Brooks hat, and they shook hands.

"You're looking good," Nicole said.

Tubby coughed out a laugh. The last time Nicole had seen him he had been hog-tied on the floor wishing he had never butted into the casino business, about to be dispatched to high-roller heaven.

"How's your nose?" Tubby asked.

Nicole blushed and fingered her face tenderly. "Very well, thank you. I'm fully recovered."

Geraldo had no idea what they were talking about, but he really did not care.

"I'm living in New Orleans now," she said. "Same place."

"Is that right?"

"Yes. Maybe we could get together and have a cup of coffee or something."

Tubby shrugged. Nicole was either the least trustworthy woman he knew or a sympathetic victim of a complicated family tragedy—he had never been sure—but she was undoubtedly good-looking.

"Got a pen?" she asked.

He did.

She wrote her number on a napkin.

"Give me a call," she suggested, and handed it to him.

"Okay." He stuffed the napkin in his jacket pocket.

He shook hands around and walked away, head awhirl again.

A Mexican woman got up from a ten-dollar blackjack table, and Tubby took her place.

When Raisin located him forty-five minutes later, he was down two hundred dollars and drunk as a judge.

chapter 34

Now that Cletus Busters was off the hook, what was bothering Tubby the most was who to take with him when he went to the dinner Mattie had planned with Dr. Byron Margolis. He gave some thought to police officer Fox Lane, but she was such a cool person that Tubby did not want to reveal to her that he had a weak spot like Mattie. He thought about the lovely Nicole Normande. The drawback there was that he might develop serious designs on her. If Jynx was right, and Margolis would make a pass at any woman Tubby liked, then it would obviously be stupid to introduce the two of them. And no telling what Mattie might do to screw things up herself. He wondered who he knew who could handle them both?

"Hello, Denise," he said when she answered. "How's it going?"

"Fine," she said. "Have you recovered from my fight?"

"Just about," he said. "I was cheering for you even if I couldn't stand to watch."

"That may be why I won."

"I hope so. Listen, would you like to have dinner with me and my ex-wife and her boyfriend tonight?"

"That sounds really great. Do I have to?"

"I'd consider it a favor. The truth is, this guy may come on to you."

"Better and better. What am I supposed to do then?"

"Just take your best shot, Denise. That's all I ask."

It was Monday, and Tubby got to the office late. He found it locked, but there were signs of Cherrylynn's presence—like a pot of hot coffee. Maybe she was taking an early lunch break.

Tubby took a chance and lit his Partagas, hoping for an hour of antisocial pleasure.

Right away, the phone rang.

"Daddy, Marcos and I have decided to get married," Debbie announced grandly.

Slowly, Tubby exhaled a long feather of smoke. Somehow this was more momentous than the fact that she was going to have a child.

"Well, that's great," he said finally. "You thought about it and decided he was up to your specifications?"

"Not quite," she said, "but he's got potential. Mainly I decided to have the baby. And I think a baby should have a father. Marcos can be trained."

"I'm happy to hear you say that. He's been in graduate school for five years now."

"He hasn't figured out yet what he wants to do."

"Fatherhood should help him."

"I suppose he can take his time. He's rich, you know."

"No, I didn't."

"Well, he is."

"It's nice to marry a rich man. Tell him to come see me."

"What for?"

"I want to talk to him."

"And say what?"

"Fathers and bridegrooms have certain things to say to each other."

"Well, don't say anything unpleasant that will scare him off."

"Oh, no. I'll be very gentle."

"Please see that you are."

"But only because he's rich."

"And I love him, too, Daddy."

"That's what I wanted to hear. Now I'll be extra gentle."

"We want to do it at the St. Charles Church."

"Are you going to make the arrangements?"

"Mother is, but she'll be talking to you about the, um, financial part."

"The what? I thought Marcos was rich."

"Well, it's traditional for the father to pay for these things. I don't want Marcos's family to think we're low-class."

"Heaven forbid he would think that. Nothing déclassé about the Dubonnets. When is the happy day?"

"As soon as possible. I don't want to be big as a house when I walk down the aisle."

After they hung up Tubby stared out the window and thought about Debbie, the infant, the child, and now what? The grown-up? There were a lot of things he wished he had done differently, he'd have to say, but he was proud about the way she was turning out. He blew a smoke ring that circled gently to the ceiling, while far below, a string of barges navigated the river's most treacherous bend.

The cigar had gone out when Tubby again picked up the telephone.

"Cletus, this is Tubby."

"Oh, hello." Tubby's client did not seem very friendly.

"I just called to congratulate you and wish you good luck."

"You did your job."

"Well, thanks, I guess. Anyway, I'm sure glad you're out of it a free man."

"I shouldn't ever have been in it."

"Yeah, well, that's true. Say, I thought we might talk."

"Can't, I'm busy right now."

Cletus hung up.

"See you around," Tubby said.

On Piety Street, Cletus went back to his favorite spot on the living room rug and sat down, cross-legged, and leaning back against the couch. He closed his eyes, trying to find his way into his trance again. Rhythmically he tossed a pair of rabbits' feet back and forth. They had little tags on them that read "Moskowitz Memorial Laboratory."

Tubby stretched and walked aimlessly around the office. In the reception area, on Cherrylynn's desk, he found a pink message slip still on the pad.

Cherrylynn had filled it up entirely with her neat handwriting.

Harold had called, it said. Collect. From Central Lockup. He had been arrested for burglary. Bond was $20,000. She had written down the docket number and the time of his arraignment. "He wants you to come and get him out," she had added.

Tubby went back to the office and stood by the window again. Balloons floated by, escaped from some child's grasp on the Moon Walk. An airplane circled the city, dragging a banner advertising a new casino on the Gulf Coast. Such innocence in such a big, bad world, he thought.

Tubby balled the pink paper up and, aiming carefully, pitched it into the trash can.

chapter 35

Cletus did not like being disturbed while he was at work. He had the feathers and sacred soils arranged just so around the candle, but the pounding on the door was so insistent he could not maintain his concentration.

He jumped up with a snarl, and throwing on a shirt to cover his painted chest, he marched angrily to the front door.

Yanking it open, he yelled, "What do you want?" at the same time he recognized Tubby Dubonnet, who took a step backwards in alarm.

"Don't shoot," Tubby said.

"Well, well," Cletus grumbled. "Why are you over here?"

"I just came by to say hello," Tubby said. "Could I come in?"

"Not just now," Cletus said gruffly. His fierce expression softened a little and he added, "Maybe some other time."

"Okay," Tubby said, disappointed. "Could you answer one question, though? How come you told Mickey O'Rourke that we didn't know the whole truth when we nailed Dr. Swincter? Did you suspect something about me being in danger?"

"I had a dream there was two snakes hanging over your bed, and you only saw one of 'em. The second one slipped under your pillow."

Tubby shuddered.

"I guess that sure explains that," he said. "Don't you ever just have a peaceful night's sleep?"

"Not too often," Cletus complained.

"I bet that could be a problem. Cletus, why in the world did you open that freezer door the night you found Dr. Valentine?"

"If it's any business of yours, which it ain't, I was looking for eyes."

"What do you mean, eyes?"

"Eyeballs, man. They had 'em in there sometimes."

"What's wrong with the ones you got?"

"They're stuck with me. I put extra eyes other places where I can see what people do."

"What for?"

"People pay me to punish the sinful. I got to find out who they is."

"How do you punish them?"

"I bring down spirits on 'em. I don't ever have to touch a hair on their heads. But they know they been visited."

Tubby watched some schoolgirls in matching blue plaid skirts and white blouses skip around the corner.

"What would you charge to drop some spirits on a man who's been slapping his girlfriend around?"

"Who is she?"

"Just a friend of mine."

Cletus thought it over. He trailed his fingernails up and down the screen door. Zip, zip, zip.

"You'd have to give me something he wears, or handles a lot."

"I could look for something like that."

"The spells shouldn't be too hard," Cletus said finally. "I'll do it pro bono. Did I say that right?"

"Hell if I know. It's Latin," Tubby said, and grinned.

•   •   •

Tubby followed Denise and Monique to a table at Sid-Mars restaurant in Bucktown. He was springing for lunch. The aroma of shrimp boiling and catfish frying, the wind off the lake, and the beer set in front of them was so intoxicating that thoughts of toil and tomorrow fled.

"We've gotta try some turtle soup," he said before the waitress could leave.

"Can we get some boiled shrimp?" Denise asked.

Two turnip-shaped men at the next table, stomachs outlined by tight red suspenders, were in serious combat with a pile of crabs, dissecting claws and sucking out the butter with precision.

"It's nice when the old places like this survive," Monique said.

"Why, are they in trouble?" Tubby asked, worried.

"No, I mean they get so much competition from those all-American restaurants. You know, Shoneys and Dennys."

"Oh," Tubby said. He hadn't noticed. "Crawfish pie is good," he told them.

"I'm going to have the crab meat salad," Denise said. "That must be full of some kind of vitamins."

They ordered and Monique told them how comfortable she was getting running the bar.

"But I'm thinking about doing something new," she said. "I may start promoting boxing matches."

"Really?" Denise exclaimed.

"Women's boxing, of course. Maybe starring Denise DiMaggio. I really think it's the coming thing."

"I'm your headliner, then." Denise laughed. "Will you excuse me a minute? Nature calls."

Monique watched her friend thread through the tables.

"She's so sweet," she said to Tubby. "And guess what! Denise has dumped her bastard boyfriend."

"That's excellent," Tubby said.

"Something has happened to her," Monique mused. "She seems stronger. Just more together."

Tubby sipped his beer.

Monique straightened her napkin. "Would you be interested," she began, "in helping me set up the fights and maybe managing some of the women?"

"I don't know anything about that," Tubby said in surprise.

"I'm sure you know a lot more than me, or any of those girls, about contracts. I think there's real money in this, and I don't want any of the kids getting ripped off."

"You know lots of these lady boxers?"

"Sure. They all come to Champs to hang, when they're not working out."

"Introduce me to some and I might get inspired." He patted his stomach. "Maybe I'd start exercising again."

Monique stared at him for a second, then half rose from her chair and leaned across the table to hug him.

"It's just always so good to see you, Tubby," she said. He was still blushing when Denise returned.

"I've almost convinced Mr. Dubonnet to be your manager," Monique proclaimed.

"I might actually need a manager," Denise said. "I'm getting some offers to fight. I'm also gonna need a new trainer."

"I'm so glad you got rid of Baxter Sharpe." Monique beamed.

"I always knew what the right decision was. It just took me a long time to make it. There's this other trainer, Franklin, that some of the girls use. He's got a better disposition than Baxter. He's bigger than Baxter, too," she added.

"You're entitled to some kindness, that's for sure."

"Baxter was sometimes nice, but it was always just a ploy, to keep me in his power."

"What did he ever do nice?" Monique demanded.

"When I cut my knuckles in that fight with Mr. Dubonnet," Denise continued, "Baxter gave me his driving gloves to wear."

"Driving gloves," Monique sneered. "Those cost about eighty-nine cents at Pep Boys."

"If your point is, he's a jerk, you're right."

Tubby ate a cracker and gazed off the porch at the seagulls resting on a row of old pilings left over from a collapsed dock, broken black spears in the flashing blue water.

"How did he take it?" Monique asked.

"Oh, he was real cracked up." Denise laughed ruefully. "Now he's gone to work on Carmella, my old sparring partner. They've already been out to Amberjacks, one of Baxter's favorite sports bars."

"Poor girl," Monique said.

"Do you still have the gloves?" Tubby asked suddenly.

"Right here," Denise said, fishing them out of her purse.

"Could I borrow them?" Tubby asked.

"What for?" Denise was surprised. Monique looked at him curiously.

" 'Sore tried and pained, the poor girl kept / Her faith, and trusted that her way, / So dark, would somewhere meet the day.' Whittier," Tubby said.

"One more time?" Monique inquired politely.

"You know I wrecked my car," Tubby said. "Maybe they'll improve my driving."

"Okay," Denise said. "I don't really have any use for them."

She handed the gloves to Tubby, who slid them off the table and into his pocket.

"The guy's a jerk," Monique repeated.

"Am I arguing with you?" Denise asked.